WILLIAM MORROW
An Imprint of HarperCollinsPublishers

I WANT MY EPIDURAL BACK

Adventures in Mediocre Parenting

KAREN ALPERT

HarperCollins books may be purchased for educational, business, or sales promotional use. For information please e-mail the Special Markets Department at SPsales@harpercollins.com.

All photographs courtesy of the author
All illustrations courtesy of Lyssa Bowen

FIRST EDITION

Designed by Janet M. Evans

Library of Congress Cataloging-in-Publication Data has been applied for.

ISBN 978-0-06-242708-3

16 17 18 19 20   OV/RRD   10 9 8 7 6 5 4 3 2 1

Dedicated to my awesome family.
I couldn't do it without you.

Then again, there's no way in hell
you could do it without me either.

Contents

Introduction

BEFORE I BECAME A MOM, I used to hear people say that having a kid is hard. I was always like, no shit, Sherlock, you're pushing an eight-pound bowling ball out something that's the size of a donut hole. And FYI, I mean the actual hole in the middle of a donut, not the delicious holes of awesomeness that are really donut *balls* and have no calories because they're so small and easy to pop in your mouth until suddenly you've eaten forty of them and you have a massive food baby. But I digress. Shit, I totally want a donut. Anyways, now that I'm a mom, I know the hardest part isn't about getting something giant through your hooha. It's about having a real live child—a one-year-old, a two-year-old, a three-year-old, a four-year-old, etc., etc., etc.

Because there might be a class that teaches you how to push and breathe and do all kinds of stuff that will help you deal with the fact that Satan is squeezing your uterus to death every four minutes, but there is NOTHING to prepare you for the pain of what comes *after* the doctor rips that epidural out of you.

Parenting is hard as shit.

Which is why sometimes I slack off. Like I order a pizza if I don't feel like cooking. Or I fish my daughter's leotard out of the hamper. Or I walk on the carpet if I have crumbs stuck to my feet. Or I give my son the iPad because he's driving me insane and I need him to STFU otherwise I might pick up the nearest sharp object and use it to stab out my eardrums. And a bunch of other shit I'm not proud of but I'm really not ashamed of either.

Because if I didn't do things half-assed then I'd have to do them full-assed, and I would probably burn out in about point two seconds. Like those crazy overachieving mommies who do stuff like offer to be the president of the PTO *AND* the vice president of the PTO because no one else wants to. Or they pack their kids' recycled lunchboxes with homegrown organic veggies that have been shaped into little designs that resemble masterpieces at the Metropolitan Museum of Art.

> **OVERACHIEVER'S KIDDO:** Oooh, look, Mommy made my kale and quinoa look like Van Gogh's *Peasant Woman Against a Background of Wheat*!!
>
> **MY RUGRAT:** Wahh, all I got is a candy bar.
>
> **OVERACHIEVER'S KIDDO:** Ohh, you poor, poor child. I'll share my flaxseed smoothie with you if you would like.
>
> **MY RUGRAT:** Bwhahahahaha, I was just bullshitting you. Snickers really satisfies. And it doesn't taste like cardboard.

Speaking of rugrats, I've got two of them. Zoey is six and she is AWWWWESOMMMMMME. I also have a three-year-old named

Holden who kicks ass. I don't mean he literally kicks ass. He's more of a hitter and a puncher. But not a biter, thank God. The last thing you want is a call from the preschool nurse telling you your kid just pulled a Mike Tyson. Anyways, I love my kiddos and without them I would be lost. On a Caribbean island lying in a hammock with a giant-ass piña colada. But as amazing as that sounds, I like my life just the way it is. Hard and loud and full of a lot of gross shit like saliva and poop and other stuff. Clearly I'm a little insane.

So there you go. I guess I could write more and include an intelligent conclusion to this profound introduction, but remember, I do things a little half-assed. So if this book sucks, that's why. Now that I've set your expectations really, *really* low, happy reading!!

Be the Best Damn
MEDIOCRE PARENT
You Can Be

I'M MEDIOCRE. NOW YOU MIGHT BE LIKE, UHHH, why would you admit that? But let me tell you something: I am damn proud of being mediocre because I'm really awesome at it. And that's no easy task. Like if you're an overachieving mom you can be all "doo doo doo doo doooooooo, I'll just hop on over to Pinterest and copy some cool shit off there and impress the socks off everyone." But there ain't no Pinterest for mediocre moms like me. Nope, there is no website to show us how to fix it when the tooth fairy forgets to come two nights in a row or how to make dinner from the contents of your fridge when it only has a stick of butter and a jar of olives and an unidentifiable tinfoil package. I mean I can't even use cookbooks. I crack one open and it says to get out your parchment paper and I'm like, WTF is parchment paper? Is that the crinkly brown paper pirates draw maps on? But here's the thing. At the end of the day, I'm doing a good enough job. At least according to my rugrats. They give me shit that says "#1 Mom" on it and I'm like, bwhahahahaha, joke's on you, I'm more like the #1,297,279 Mom. But they truly think I'm the best mom on earth. And that's all that matters.

You might be a mediocre mom if . . .

You can hear the word "Mommy" sixteen times before reacting.

You know the frozen pizza goes in at 400°F for 19 to 22 minutes without looking at the instructions.

You think pretty much anything your kid's wearing is acceptable as long as it covers the genitals.

You know the best organic cleaning fluid is saliva.

You can gather lunch for your children from the contents of your car floor.

You make the kids sleep in their clothes if you're going somewhere early the next morning.

You would take your coffee intravenously if it were an option. And your vodka.

You find yourself sitting at the PTO meeting wondering WTF you've gotten yourself into.

You can stealthily bury the kids' artwork in the trash can while they are sitting in the same room.

You do the laundry in cold water because who the hell has time to separate whites from colors?

You sometimes eat the Cheerios that fall out of your bra when you get undressed at night because it's easier than walking alllllll the way to the trash can.

You lie to your children's dentist every ~~6 months~~ ~~12 months~~ 18 months.

You've failed miserably at doing at least one Pinterest project.

You haven't gotten a single photo printed in years.

You accidentally wear your slippers out of the house and realize it when you're in the garage but don't go back inside to change them because who gives a shit.

You don't have time to take showers every day (or even every other day sometimes) and just use baby wipes on the stinky parts.

You use your *microwave* oven more than your *oven* oven.

You don't have a 5-second rule. You have a 5,000-second rule.

You have to stack dirty dishes next to the sink because it's already overflowing with dirty dishes.

You write stuff on your to-do list that you've already done so you feel productive.

You cook three-course dinners, but only because no one in your family will eat the same thing.

You couldn't braid your daughter's hair to save your life, but you can totally braid your leg hair.

You have to ask if your kids can get a different Happy Meal toy because they already have that one.

You kick ass at being a parent even though some people think you don't. And if you're one of those people, F off and die. No wait, don't die. That's totally mean. Just F off.

HOLDEN: Mommy, can you blow me?

I can't begin to tell you how relieved I was when I looked up and he was holding a tissue. Holy crap, heart attack averted.

Girl Scout troop leaders F'ing rock, which is exactly why I shouldn't be one

OKAY, SO THERE ARE MOMS who organize shit like fund-raisers and book drives and other annoying important stuff, and then there are moms who organize shit like MNOs. If you don't know what that is, go look it up. Whoops, never mind, I just Googled it and Google says MNO stands for Money News Online, Mobile Network Operator, and some random inorganic chemical compound. Yo Google, I usually think you're like a total genius but today you are wrong. MNO stands for Moms' Night Out. Only like the most important thing on earth.

Those PTO moms might feel all superior and shit for organizing their big ol' bake sales, but the way I see it, they're just making a profit off getting people fat. When I organize an MNO, I am single-handedly saving the planet because moms are like the most important people on earth and if we don't occasionally get a break where we can drink a little vino and bitch about our problems to each other, we will literally go insane and all be thrown into an insane asylum and the planet will go to shit.

So a few weeks before Zoey started kindergarten, I sent an e-mail out to all the other kindergarten moms inviting them to an MNO. Here it is, paraphrased:

Dear slutbags (I can call you that because for the next thirteen years our rugrats are going to be in school together and we're going to become good friends),

Instead of all of us meeting in the carpool line and only talking to the people we already know and then some people don't know anyone and they feel like outcast losers for the next thirteen years, let's get together for a beer or four so we can meet each other when we're a little less sober and a little more buzzed so it isn't as awkward. Here's the info of when and where we'll meet, blah blah blah blah blah.

Love,

A mom who's looking forward to your having my kiddo over for lots of playdates because she's perfect and always well behaved despite what you may have heard

Anyways, the night of the big MNO I wonder what to wear but then I realize it doesn't matter because who the hell am I trying to impress? I'm going to be with other moms who are pretty much only going to see me wearing pajamas in the carpool line for the next thirteen years. I get to the bar right at 7 p.m., because I'm the organizer and I have to show up on time and that sucks because I have to sit down at a table all alone and wait. And wait. And wait.

And pray to the beer gods that I am not the only one who shows up to my own event. And then someone walks in. And then some more people. And then the whole F'ing class of totally badass moms. Wahooooo!!! People came! I'm not a total loser!! At least not for this reason.

So we talk about our kiddos and our fears about them starting kindergarten and we share our stories about giving birth because MNO conversations always include stories about giving birth for some reason, and within an hour I know which moms gave birth naturally and which ones used drugs (aka which ones I'll probably be friends with), and by hour two I'm having a conversation with a woman who chose not to have an epidural who's either very strong, has a very stretchy vagina, or is clinically insane.

OTHER WOMAN: I was thinking about starting a Girl Scout troop for their class.

ME: Oh, that's a great idea! I loved being a Girl Scout.

OTHER WOMAN: Do you want to do it with me?

ME: Sure!

If you've read this book chronologically (holy crap is that a hard word to type) and didn't just randomly open it to this page, you're probably like, WTF? You're probably wondering why on earth I would think it is any of my business being a Girl Scout troop leader. Well, I can answer you in one word. Beer. Duh. Isn't alcohol the reason we commit to pretty much everything in life?

RANDOM GUY: Will you go home with me?

ME: Sure!

Beer's fault.

HUBBY: Will you marry me?

ME: Yes!

Beer again.

ME: Whoopsies, I'm preggers!!

Beer.

WOMAN: Do you want to be a Girl Scout troop leader with me?

ME: Sure!

Beeeeeer.

Because I know it seems like an innocent question, but if you read between the lines, this is what she was really asking:

OTHER WOMAN: Do you want to be a troop leader and be responsible for twenty loud kindergarten girls and do all sorts of things outside of your comfort zone, like come up with annoying Pinterest-y projects at the last minute and iron badges on uniforms and stand in a circle holding hands and singing stupid songs and stand outside the supermarket selling cookies to random strangers in the freezing cold and then deliver those cookies to the strangers and use all of your willpower not to eat their boxes of cookies before you deliver them?

ME: Sure!

Beer. Beer. Beer. Beer. Four bottles, to be exact.

I mean I kind of want to call up this mom today and be like, FU, you totally tricked me into becoming a Girl Scout troop leader because you knew I was drunk and more likely to say yes. But the truth is, all she knew was that I was the mom who organized this big MNO and probably thought I was the kind of person who organizes shit, when really the only kind of stuff I organize is events where people drink together so I don't have to drink alone.

So now I'm roped in for a year. Ennnnh, wrong again. I just finished my first year and now realize I'm actually roped in for FIVE more years because if I quit now, Zoey's gonna say shit like, "Mom, why did you stop being my Girl Scout leader?" and "Do you still love me?" and make me feel like the worst mom on earth. So Girl Scouts is basically a SIX-year sentence!!! AGGHHHHHHH!!!!

Anyways, don't get me wrong, it's not all that bad. Like last week we did this super-fun project where the kids tied fleece together to make pillows. And this is how it went.

ME: Okay, so you take these two pieces of fleece and you tie them together.

GIRL SCOUT: I don't know how to tie.

GIRL SCOUT: Me neither.

GIRL SCOUT: Help me!

ME: Girls, watch here. You take this strand and you wrap it around this one and then you poke it through the hole.

Awwww shit, I look up and a sea of confused faces are staring back at me from the table like *huhhh???*

ME: Okay, let's try it this way. So you cross this one over this one, make this little hole, and then pop the little bunny through his hole.

GIRL SCOUT: I like bunnies!

GIRL SCOUT: Me too!

GIRL SCOUT: Bunnies are so cute.

ME: Awesome.

GIRL SCOUT: Miss Karen, I can't do it!!

GIRL SCOUT: Help me!!!

GIRL SCOUT: Noooo, help me FIRST!!!!! AGGGHHHHHH!!!!!

GIRL SCOUTS AROUND THE WORLD: Wahhhhh, helllppppppppp meeeeeee!!!! I'm going to scream and cry unless you stop what you are doing right now and come help us all at the same time!!

And in a matter of seconds the entire table is freaking out and begging me to help them, but I'm not an F'ing octopus so they all start losing it and tears are rolling down their faces and now they're crying even more because their projects are getting wet from all the tears and thanks, Pinterest, this project is really fun! Oh, and I should also mention that my son, Holden, is also screaming to me from across the room because hell if I'm spending $20 for a babysitter every meeting, so he has to come to Girl Scouts with me every week. See?

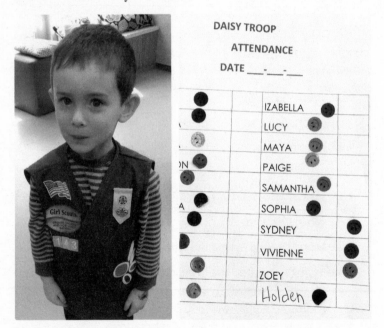

DAISY TROOP

ATTENDANCE

DATE ___-___-___

	IZABELLA			
	LUCY			
	MAYA			
	PAIGE			
	SAMANTHA			
	SOPHIA			
	SYDNEY			
	VIVIENNE			
	ZOEY			
	Holden			

And now his iPad has conveniently run out of batteries at the same time that all the girls are freaking out and he's shitting a brick because F'ing *PAW Patrol* stopped in the middle and he's nevvverrrr going to find out whether Chase and Ryder save the stupid hoedown or the walrus or whatever annoying *PAW Patrol* episode he's watching. Sorry, *PAW Patrol*, I love you. You take care of my kiddos all the time, but this is what I do in stressful situations—I take shit out on my loved ones. And you, *PAW Patrol*, are definitely a loved one.

Anyways, like a million minutes later, I've finished tying as many pillows as I can for the girls and my fingers have gone into arthritic (is that even a word???) shock and all the girls (and Holden) are sitting in a circle on the rug and we're singing the same adorable song we sing every time.

> *Make new friends, but keep the old,*
> *One is silver and the other's gold.*

Only here's what's going through my head:

> *Don't make new friends, new friends suck,*
> *Because they don't know who you are and they ask you*
> *to do shitty things like be the Girl Scout troop leader*
> *when you're drunk.*

Yeah, I know it doesn't rhyme and it has way too many syllables, but that's just the way I do things. The wrong way. Which is exactly why people like me should never be Girl Scout troop leaders.

I don't know WTF everyone's talking about.
I didn't have any problem putting the patches on
Zoey's vest.

I became a mom because I drank too much.
Now I drink too much because I'm a mom.

Shit I do that
I know I shouldn't do

YEAH, I'M THAT MOM. Sometimes I do shit because it's easier or cheaper or just because it's more fun. Am I worried about the well-being of my kiddos? Sure. Sometimes. But I'm also worried about my own well-being. And if I listened to every overachieving Martha Stewart-y a-hole who looks down her nose at me, I'd probably slit my wrists, and *that* wouldn't be healthy at all. So here goes. A bunch of shit I do that I know I shouldn't do but I do anyways because life is too short to worry so much.

1. I take my kids to McDonald's. GASP!!! A lot. And damn does that shit taste good. I mean yeah, I know it's mostly chemicals, but somewhere in there there's a real potato, right? It's not like the scientists are standing in a lab putting a bunch of chemicals together and suddenly they're like, "KABLOOEY, there's a French fry!"

2. I let the TV babysit them. I mean every month I get the cable bill and I'm like, holy crap, you want *how* much?!!! And then

I'm like, ohhh, I guess that's not so bad. I just got a full-time nanny for $120 a month!

3. I don't buy organic shit. Hellllllo, do you know what organic shit does? It goes bad in like negative three seconds. And here's another reason I don't buy organic. It costs like a million dollars. I mean I'm standing in the store going, hmmmm, which strawberries should I buy? The ones that are $2.99 and are plump and red and juicy? Or the ones that are $5.99 and look like dried cranberries?

4. I let my kids wear whatever the hell they want as long as they aren't going to freeze to death or be mistaken for a hooker.

5. I let my kids eat dirt. And suck on banisters. And eat crusty old Cheerios off the floor in the car. I mean it's not like I say, "Go eat dirt," but I don't react as quickly as I should. Like last week Holden was licking the elevator buttons and I didn't react for at least ten floors. In my defense, a really cute UPS guy got on so I was a little distracted. You should have seen his package.

6. Speaking of dirt, here are my two favorite cleaning products: saliva and 409. First I use saliva, and if it doesn't do the job I get off my lazy ass and go get the 409. So pretty much every

surface in my house is either crawling with my mouth bacteria or will make your genes mutate. Want to come over for dinner?

7. If I suddenly realize that my kiddo forgot to change his underwear that morning, I tell him to change it. Unless he already has his shoes on. Then I say we'll just change it as soon as he gets home from school, only I usually forget after school and finally remember right before he goes to bed and why would he put on a clean pair of underwear just to go to bed? No wonder his ass smells like ass.

8. And speaking of asses that smell like asses, I don't bathe my kiddos every night. I mean hell if I'm letting my kids sit back and take a luxurious bubble bath when I'm lucky to squeeze in a shower two mornings a week. And if *anyone* needs a shower, it's the person whose arms were licked up and down even though she kept yelling, "*Lick Mommy* is NOT a funny game!"

9. I dream about my kids becoming nerds. That's right. I see all these moms clambering to get their kids into the popular clique and I'm like, are you crazy??? Do you know what popular kids do? BJ rings and coke. Do you know what nerdy kids do? Study and stay home with their parents on Saturday nights. I mean no, I don't want them to be so nerdy that they get held up by their underpants and get thrown into lockers and shit, but a little nerdy would be awesome. Of course, this may be unlikely considering how cool their parents are. Bwhahahahahaha.

10. I don't finish shit.

ZOEY: *Mommy, I need you . . .*

ME: *Awww, that's so sweet, honey.*

ZOEY: *. . . to buy me that Lego set.*

WTF? How was I supposed to know she'd insert a giant pause into her sentence?

A love letter to another mediocre mom

Dear Future BFF,

Oh, how I've dreamed of meeting you for so many years. The fantasy plays out in my head time and time again. I'm sitting in a restaurant and I hear a ruckus across the room because your rugrat is filling his soda cup, only he won't stop and the soda is overflowing and you've lost your shit and now you're threatening to lock him in the car. I swoon because we are so alike.

Your greasy hair is pulled back into a half-assed ponytail that's falling out, there are deep-set wrinkles under your eyes from years of being tortured by children throughout the night, and your beautiful butt looks like it has four butt cheeks because your underwear is too tight and is cutting each butt cheek in half under your disgusting faded black leggings that are your favorites because they're the only ones that fit you anymore. I am stunned by your beauty.

I can tell that we are meant for each other by the way you chug your wine like you're drinking Gatorade at the end of a marathon and shovel fistfuls of leftover French fries and pizza crusts from your kid's plate into your pie hole even though "technically" you're just having a salad.

And even when my kid is making piercing dolphin noises that might break the glass windows, you smile at me, and not one of those jackass condescending smiles. The kind of smile that says, "Been there, done that, and I know how much it sucks to be you." Because you are me. And I am you.

As you struggle to get your kid to put his coat on, I have plenty of time to come up to you, but alas, I'm too busy prying the salt-shaker out of my kid's hands before it spills everywhere because he unscrewed the top. And then when I look up, you're gone.

Out the window, I see you opening the door to your minivan and my heart swells as you hold piles of trash and toys in your car before it spills out. And after you finally wrestle your little jackass into his car seat by pushing down on his crotch (which I know from experience feels really wrong) and are about to pull out of the parking spot, you remember one more thing.

You jump out and run up to the window where I'm sitting and you slam something against the glass so I can see it. It's a dried-up crusty old wipe with your phone number scrawled across it.

I ignore my kid and text you before you even pull out of the parking lot and we plan a playdate for Monday morning. Wine included. It is fate and we will be friends forever.

Love,
Another mediocre mom

I just stole the batteries from my kid's toy to put in my own "toy." I feel like I've reached a new low, and yet I'm feeling very, VERY good.

FRIEND: *I can make reservations for tonight. Does seven thirty work?*

ME: *How about seven?*

FRIEND: *Oh, you want to go BEFORE the kids go to bed?*

ME: *It's either that or I lie to my husband and tell him you're picking me up at seven and hide behind a tree for a half hour in the front yard waiting for you 'cause I don't want to deal with putting the kids to bed.*

A completely unscientific study about multitasking

AGGGHHH, I HAVE LIKE 9 MILLION THINGS TO DO and there aren't even 9 million seconds in a day. I don't know how the hell I'm gonna get it all done. Oh wait, I know! I'll multitask. Nahhh, not like I'm gonna check my e-mails while I'm watching the kids beat the shit out of each other. Anyone can check their phone while they're doing other stuff. I mean like I'm *REALLY* gonna come up with some inventive ways to multitask. If I can save myself a few minutes in a day, I might actually get in a shower this week. If not, back the F up because one lift of my arm and my BO is literally going to make your nose shrivel up and die. Be back soon to report my findings.

Okay, I'm back! And boy, did I learn a lot. I mean yeah, some of my new multitasking ideas were awesome and saved me tens of seconds, but some of them were total failures. I'd be a complete a-hole if I didn't share these life-changing scientific results with you, so here goes:

Peeing While You Brush Your Teeth

Okay, yeah, so I've never actually tried this one (total lie) but here's why I think it would be awesome. You're brushing your teeth, you quickly sit to pee, you keep brushing your teeth, and voilà! You just saved yourself thirty seconds. I mean yeah, you have to be okay with the toothbrush being exposed to the pee-pee particles floating in the air, but if your ass is as big as mine, it covers up the toilet hole anyway and there really aren't any toilet particles floating out. And if your ass is skinny and doesn't cover the whole bowl, then I kinda hate you a little and don't care if toilet particles get on your toothbrush. Shit, did I just say that out loud? Please note, I said PEEING. It is NOT okay to do this if you are pooping because (a) that's disgusting, and (b) if your mouth is minty and on fire you'll have to prematurely pinch the loaf to get to the sink to spit.

SCIENTIFIC CONCLUSION FOR PEEING: WIN
SCIENTIFIC CONCLUSION FOR POOPING: FAIL

Doing *Other* Stuff While You Brush Your Teeth

Okay, seriously, how the hell am I supposed to get everything done in the morning before school AND have good hygiene? Hmmm, what if I brush my teeth at the same time I'm getting dressed? Ennnhhh, bad idea. Because then I can either get dressed with my left hand, which takes twice as long because I suck at using my left hand, or I can brush my teeth with my left hand and end up jabbing myself in the cheek over and over again and then miss my mouth completely and get a streak of toothpaste down the side of my face, which ends up taking extra precious seconds to clean. Or I totally forget I'm even brushing my teeth at all and the toothbrush lies dormant in my mouth while I put my panties on and all I've done is let my teeth marinate in Colgate for the past five minutes. And why the hell did I just use the word "panties"? Ewwww. Sorry.

SCIENTIFIC CONCLUSION: FAIL

Thinking About Important Shit While You're Having Sex with Your Hubby

Last night my hubby was basically a man in heat and I was like, I would lovvvve to have sex with you right now but do you know how much shit I have going on? No can do. And then I realized that if "too busy" were a legitimate excuse, we would never do it. So hey, here's an idea. What if I could do something else at the same time and kill two penises with one stone? (I promise, honey, it's just a saying.) Like come up with options for my kid's science experiment. Or figure out a Girl Scout project for our meeting on Wednesday. Or think about what I'm cooking for dinner this week. "Yes, YES, Mexican lasagna, that's it!! Oh my God, right there!! With guacamole!" And if you think my hubby would be offended if he knew I was multitasking, so what? "Honey, would you rather have sex with me while I'm thinking about something else or would you rather not have sex at all?" Yeah, that's what I thought. Plus, if I'm thinking about our dinner menu, then I can't be thinking about Channing Tatum, right? I mean hypothetically speaking, of course.

SCIENTIFIC CONCLUSION: WIN

Blowing My Nose When I'm Doing the Laundry

So I'm gathering the kids' dirty clothes together so I can do the eighth load of laundry this week when my nose starts to run. I mean sure, it would only take about 20 seconds to stop and get a tissue, but remember, that's a third of a minute and that shit adds up. I know what I can do. I mean all this laundry is getting washed anyways, so can't I just grab something from the hamper and use it like a hanky? Brilliant!!! Until I bury my nose into a piece of clothing and realize it's the butt of Holden's pajamas and I just got a noseful of dookie smell. Awesome.

SCIENTIFIC CONCLUSION: FAIL

Okay, okay, by now you get the picture and you're probably like, STFU already, so here are a few more quick ones to help you make the right multitasking decisions throughout your day.

Putting Your Kid's Shoes on While He's on the Toilet

Particularly awesome, because my kid always says he has to poop the second we're heading out the door. Every. F'ing. Time.

SCIENTIFIC CONCLUSION: WIN

Talking on the Phone While You're Doing a Target Run

Have you ever seen people who do this? They basically look like zombies walking around Target picking up random items and pretending to look at the items when really they're focused on their phone conversation and it doubles the amount of time they spend there. Plus, they end up with a bunch of random shit in their cart and their bill at the cash register is $900 instead of $700, when really they only came in for toothpaste in the first place.

SCIENTIFIC CONCLUSION: FAIL

Calling Someone While You're Getting a Pap Smear

SCIENTIFIC CONCLUSION: FAIL FOR OBVIOUS REASONS

Chugging Hershey's Syrup While Cooking Dinner

The way I see it, I'm not ruining my appetite by doing this. I'm just multitasking so I don't have to waste all that time eating dessert later. Bwhahahahaha, like I'm not gonna have a second dessert at 9 p.m. And a third right before I head upstairs to bed.

SCIENTIFIC CONCLUSION: WIN!!!!!!!!

(Side note, do you see me doing this without getting a stream of chocolate on my face? This is a serious skill that has taken me years to master. Seriously, try it. And that's an order.)

So that's about it. I'll bet you're like wayyyy smarter than I am and can come up with some even brillianter ways to multitask and save yourself all sorts of awesome time. You're welcome, and good luck!!

Sometimes instead of pushing 2:00 on the microwave, I push 2:22 because then I don't waste time pushing multiple buttons. Yes, this is the kind of shit I think about.

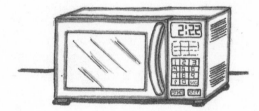

Twenty-eight ways being a mom is like being in prison

1. You never get to poop alone.

2. Conjugal visits are few and far between.

3. Someone is ALWAYS watching you.

4. You pretty much wear the same thing every day.

5. You wash other people's dirty clothes all day long.

6. You are surrounded by crazy people.

7. Sometimes you think YOU are going crazy.

8. You're often subjected to unexpected pat downs.

9. You never get to sleep alone.

10. It's not unusual to hear screaming and/or crying in the middle of the night.

11. Someone else dictates when you wake up every morning.

12. You've lowered your standards big time when it comes to food.

13. Your showers have to be fast and furious.

14. There are never enough toilets for everyone.

15. Someone else decides what you watch on TV.

16. You often stare out the window longing to be somewhere else.

17. Visitors don't really understand what you're going through.

18. You don't really know what's going on in the outside world.

19. If you bend over, you are likely to be poked inappropriately.

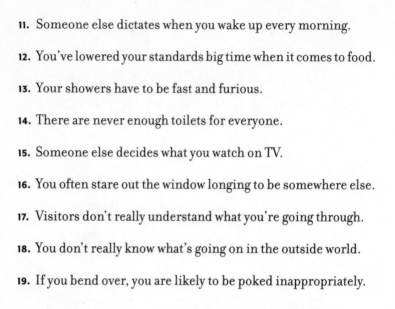

20. You really look forward to getting the mail every day.

21. You barely get to wear makeup anymore.

22. People do gross things like smear poop on the walls.

23. You often count down the number of years you have left.

24. You're constantly walking on eggshells trying not to piss anyone off.

25. You worry about someone getting hold of a sharp object.

26. You find yourself guarding your genitals a lot.

27. You're coming to terms with being someone else's bitch.

28. You often wonder how you got yourself into this mess.

You're born and then you die, and if you're a parent,
somewhere in the middle you go to hell.

Tell Those
Overachieving Moms
TO SUCK IT

OKAY, SO HERE'S THE DEALIO. I'M NOT TOO JUDG-
mental when it comes to other moms. You do what you wanna do when it comes to parenting. But duuuuuude, calm the F down. Do you seriously need to paint every kid's first, middle, and last names in rainbow colors on the super-special party favors that each cost more than the crappy birthday present my kid brought to the party? And in case you're wondering, yeah, that's ours, the one that's wrapped in two different kinds of wrapping paper. Because (a) I was stoopid and bought a gift that wouldn't fit into a gift bag from the Dollar Store, and (b) I only had a small amount of two different kinds of wrapping paper left. And yes, I know that one of them is Hanukkah paper. And yes, I know that it's July. And yes, I know that you are Christian. And no, I don't give a shit. Because parenting is hard enough without a bunch of overachieving mommies rubbing it in our faces on Facebook and Pinterest and in the carpool line every day. Anyways, PTO presidents and Pinterest divas, this section's for you. Or rather, against you.

Only a-holes
send chain letters

SO THE OTHER DAY I'M SITTING in the kitchen when I hear the most beauteous sound ever. The squeak of the mailbox opening. "The mail is here! The mail is here!" I run around the living room in circles like a dog. I mean it's not like I'm expecting anything special, but for some reason when you're at home allllll day long taking care of your little crotchmuffins, you get excited when the mail comes—yeah, even though it's just filled with shit like bills and coupon books and two Pottery Barn catalogs (seeeeriously, does your computer system suck that bad that it can't see that you are sending TWO catalogs to ONE address?) and another catalog called Oriental Trading (ummm, is it just me or does that sound like an Asian slave-trading catalog?).

So I grab the mail and start sifting through it. Bill, bill, junk mail, bill, hmm, I wonder what this one is. It's addressed to my kiddo. I guess I should probably wait till she gets home from kindergarten to open it, but F that. She's only five and it looks interesting so I'll open it for her.

(I'm too lazy to type the whole letter out so I'm going to para-phrase it a little.)

Dear Zoey,

This is a chain letter and you have to send some stickers to the first person on this page and then copy this page and move the second person into the first person's place [I've now read that line eight times and I still don't know WTF it's telling me to do] and then add your name and address and photocopy it and send it to six of your friends, but not the same friends who already got it and since you don't have many friends yet because you're only five, you're going to have to dig deep to figure out some new people to send it to, and by the way, you're gonna have to get your mom to do alllllllll of this for you because you can't do jack shit yet because you're only five. And if you don't do this, you're going to have bad luck for seven years. And then in four weeks you'll be so excited when you get a stupid sheet of Dora the Explorer stickers in the mail, even though you hate Dora, from some random person you don't know.

> *Love,*
> *A friend who apparently hates your mom*
> *and thinks she has lots of downtime*

Anyways, my point is this. I am soooooo sick of this chain let-ter crap that I don't even do it anymore. That's right, that letter you so carefully photocopied to send out from your kiddo? I tore that shit up and threw it in the trash. Not even the recycling bin because that shit has some seriously bad juju and I don't want it being recycled into toilet paper or something and spreading its bad juju to someone's good hooha.

And yeah, I know I suck because now your kid is sitting there four weeks later wondering why her sixth pack of stickers hasn't arrived (ennnnh, bullshit because kids don't remember things four weeks later, or even four hours later, unless it's the lollipop I got from the bank and put in my purse, in which case kids remember that kinda stuff forevvvvver). So F the moms who think chain letters are cute and perpetuate this bullshit tradition. In fact, here you go. I wrote my own little chain letter that I will be sending out to some of my "favorite" moms tonight.

Dear mom who sent me a chain letter from your rugrat,

This is another adorable chain letter. It is being sent to you because your child (really you) sent my child (really me) a chain letter, so I can tell that you think chain letters are super fun. Here's how this one works. Photocopy the following message and send it to seven of your best overachieving mom friends:

Chain letters SUCCCCCCCK and are super annoying and moms don't have time for irritating shit like that, so stop doing it.

If you do not do send this to seven people, you will be cursed forever and die.

Sincerely,
When my kiddo is old enough to do chain letters
without my help, then you may send her one

You know how all those Missy McPerfects brag on Facebook about their perfect kiddos? Well, I apologize, but I'm gonna join them for a moment. My kid doesn't just say I love you—he pees it in a heart shape on the carpet. Try not to be jealous.

FRIEND: *There's an opening on the PTO. Would you have any interest?*

ME: *I don't know. How much does it pay?*

FRIEND: *Nothing.*

ME: *Do I get a certificate or a trophy or something?*

FRIEND: *Umm, no.*

ME: *Are your kids really proud of you for being on it?*

FRIEND: *I don't think they even know what it is.*

ME: *So why do you do it?*

FRIEND: *Ummm—*

ME: *Wait, I know. You're on the PTO so people like me don't have to be on the PTO.*

A bunch of things I do that make overachieving moms think I'm a shitty mom, and maybe they're right but I don't care

1. I let my rugrats ride on the bottom of the shopping cart. And yes, Muffy McPrissypants, I know that's how fingers get mangled. Side note, do not Google images of mangled fingers. I don't know why I just did that. Holy crap. But even after seeing those pictures, I will *still* let my kids ride under the cart. Only now I'll just yell at them even louder to "GET YOUR F'ING HANDS AWAY FROM THE F'ING WHEELS BEFORE YOU LOSE A FINGER!!!!!"

2. Screen time? WTF is screen time? That's bullshit. There's iPad time and there's TV time and there's iPhone time and there's Wii time. That way, I can plop her in front of the TV and then after she's watched a couple of shows I move her to the iPad and then while I'm cooking dinner I let her play the Wii. I mean TV is where she can veg out, and the Wii is where she gets good hand-eye coordination, and the iPad is where she learns important shit like math and reading, even though really all she does is play stupid princess dress-up games.

3. You know those itty-bitty carrots and celery that come in a can of chicken noodle soup? Voilà, veggies are served. Yeah, I know those are totally bullshit and they don't really count because (a) they're like the size of an atom, and (b) if my kids notice them they FA-REAK out and gag like their tongues are made of vomit and refuse to eat any of the soup until the miniature Barbie veggies are removed. But seriously, who has time to cook a whole dish of veggies that their kids aren't gonna eat anyways? The way I see it, by not cooking a veggie I'm NOT wasting food, so I'm basically helping starving children all over the world.

4. ME: Holden, wash your hands after you go potty.

HOLDEN: No.

ME: Okay.

Yeah, I know I'm supposed to teach him to wash his hands every time, but it's just such a pain in the ass. Plus, he's just gonna touch his butt again anyways.

5. Whenever I can't think of what to make for lunch, I pack the kids in the car and take them to Costco, where there is an abundance of free samples. And then when we find an awesome sample, like chocolate clusters, we "accidentally" walk down the same aisle a few times.

"Why yes, we would love to try some chocolate."

"Oooh, that chocolate looks good. Could we have a taste?"

"Nooo, we haven't tried this chocolate yet. We're just the kind of people who look like a lot of other people."

"You have to give us another taste. It's the Costco law."

6. Sometimes (translation: all the time) when the kids are fighting downstairs, I yell at them to "work it out." It's a superimportant skill they need to develop. Plus, I just don't feel like getting up and walking all eighteen steps to the playroom. So far no deaths or brain injuries!

7. I never correct Holden when he mispronounces stuff because I think it's cute that he calls flamingo "flingo" and nail polish "paint nolish" and *hasta luego* "enchilado" and even says cute things like "the cat is throw-upping." And sometimes I even make him say it over and over again so I can hear it the wrong way. What's the cat doing? Wait, what did you say he's doing? I forgot, say it again.

8. I let Zoey skip practicing her reading words all the time. I mean yeah, sometimes I just forget, but sometimes I'm like, ugggh, doing flashcards is sooooo painful and slow and then she gets mad at me for making her try and then I end up yelling at her. Oh well, so she'll be illiterate. There are worse things. And at least we won't fight as much so I'll always be there to read everything to her.

9. Once or twice a week I pretend like I have the runs at exactly the same time we're supposed to leave the house so my hubby has to deal with getting the kids' shoes and coats on while I go hide out in the bathroom and read *People* magazine. Not for too long. Just until I hear the back door slam. Then I come out. Honey, if you're reading this, I made that one up. I don't really do that.

Dear lady who condescendingly looks at me with pity every time I drop my kid off at school and he screams and cries his eyes out while your kid walks in all nicely,

I just wanted to let you know that the reason my kid cries and yours doesn't is because mine loves me more and can't stand to be away from me because I'm so F'ing awesome.

Sincerely,
My kid misses me. Does yours?

Yo douchebags who constantly brag on Facebook, this chapter's for you

OMG, SO THE OTHER DAY I waxed my mustache and it took off a little skin and then I spent the rest of the morning cleaning semi-dry throw-up out of the cracks in Holden's floor, so I was feeling a little depressed. I have no idea why—my life is like totally glamorous. Anyways, I had approximately thirteen minutes until carpool pickup and I said to myself, "I'm gonna relax for those thirteen minutes and just surf Facebook and catch up with my virtual friends who I haven't talked to in decades but we think we're still friends because we spy on each other through social media." Ennnnnh. Bad move.

Because here's what you should NOT do when you are depressed. Go on Facebook. Facebook is basically a cesspool of perfect people showing off their perfect lives and their perfect children.

Do you have people like that in your newsfeed? Ooooooh, look at my big house. Ooooooh, look at the fabulous vacation we're on. Ooooooh, look at my perfect kids who are so well behaved. Ooooooh, look at the group of women who I went out with tonight and you weren't invited. I mean no, they don't just come right out and say, "Look how amazing my child is!!!" But they'll say something like, "Does anyone know what the best kind of shoes are for my eight-month-old who's already walking?" Some people call this a "humble brag." But I call it "you'd have to be an idiot not to know this person is showing off."

Do you know the Facebook posts I'm talking about? Here are some examples. Oh, and just for shits and giggles (and because it'll make me feel better), I'm gonna add what I wish I had the balls to write in the comments section.

Megan: Sorry to post another picture of my boys today. They're just so cute, I can't resist.

My comment: Thank God you did. I was just thinking that eleven pictures in one day is not enough.

Lisa: The teacher just called to tell me Madison is the only one in her class who can write her letters!

My comment: She's bullshitting you. My kid can write *F* and *U*.

Jessica: Oh nooo, today Cambria went on a playdate and the mom took the girls to McDonald's and Cambria called it an UN-Happy Meal and refused to taste it because I taught her that McDonald's is really unhealthy. My bad!

My comment: WTF kind of name is Cambria? Did you steal that from a Pottery Barn Kids catalog?

Bree: My husband and I are arguing and we need some advice. Do you think it's okay to fly with little kids in first class, or does one of us need to sit in coach with them?

My comment: I think he should take me since we're sleeping together.

My second comment a minute or two later: Just kidding.

My third comment: One of you probably needs to sit back with the peasants. Wear brown burlap so you don't stand out.

Emily: Oh noooo, baby Hudson is crawling at seven months and he's getting into everything!! If your child isn't crawling yet, don't feel bad. Feel lucky!

My comment: Studies show that babies who crawl first are often first to do other things. Like smoke pot and lose their virginity.

Abigail: I'm super proud of myself for being so crafty! I went on Pinterest and picked out all the things I wanted to do for Whitlington's birthday and then I sent them to the party planner.

My comment: Who should I give my RSVP to? You or the party planner? Ennh, I'll just put it here: No F'ing way.

Rachel: Totally bummed. I made homemade chocolate chip cookies, but Eloise wouldn't stop eating my homemade kale chips and now she's too full for dessert. Ping me if you want the recipe.

My comment: F the recipe. Just drop the chocolate mouthgasms off at my house.

Melanie: Ugggh, the maid taught Reginald all this Spanish and I can't understand a word he's saying. Now I totally know what it's like to have a child with a speech problem.

My comment: Can you please ask him how to say the word *douchebag* in Spanish?

Pamela: I'm so jealous of all these moms who wear pajamas to drop the kids off at school. I wear little nighties to bed, so I have to put on real clothes every morning.

My comment: Do you pull that stick out of your ass every morning too?

Jenny: Wahhh, I want a funny school picture like everyone else is posting, but my little Mattelyne just can't seem to take a bad picture. See?

My comment: You spelled her name wrong.

Lauren: I made little goodie bags for all the people sitting around us on the airplane in case my kids misbehaved, but of course they acted like total angels the whole flight. Murphy's Law. Oh well, guess they'll have to find another reason to use the earplugs!

My comment: Surely there was someone else they wanted to stop listening to.

Anyways, maybe you're thinking I'm just jealous of all these people and their perfect lives. Well, yes, if their lives *really* are this perfect, I'm absolutely jealous. But I don't believe it for a sec. Because when a mom has to brag this much, you just kinda know something's missing from her life. Like maybe her husband is missing because he's on a "business trip" diddling his coworker. Or maybe a stick is missing from the garden because it's stuck up her butt. But here's the thing. My life is pretty damn good. Not perfect, but good enough. I just don't feel the need to constantly broadcast it.

Once upon a time there was this woman who stabbed someone to death and then the police were after her, so she grabbed her kids, hot-wired a car, and took off for Mexico, and as soon as they crossed the border she pulled over for a pee break and before they got back in the car she said, "Say cheese," and she took an adorable picture of them on the beach and then posted it to Facebook with the caption "Beautiful sunset tonight!!" and everyone who saw it just assumed they were having the most wonderful vacation in Mexico.

See, Facebook lies.

But all you did on your birthday was slide out my hooha

SO LET ME GET THIS straight. I pushed an eight-pound bowling ball out my hooha and *who* gets to celebrate every year on that date? The F'ing bowling ball??? Yeahhh, that makes sense. Not.

There are some moms who are practically jizzing in their pants, they're so F'ing excited to plan their kid's birthday. They're like, "Eeeeks, I only have three hundred sixty-four days to plan little Poopiebottom's birthday party!! Must go to Pinterest NOWWW." Which is the complete opposite of me. I'm like, "Seriously? Seeeriously? We are going to drop how many hundreds of dollars on a party that's going to last one-and-three-quarter hours and literally be forgotten the next day?" For moms like me who are busy and lazy and not rich, there is nothing more torturous on this planet than planning a birthday party. Maybe waterboarding. Nahh, I'm gonna say it's a tie.

Anyways, every year I DREAD the conversation. I mean when Zoey was little, I got to pick where we were doing it.

Age 1: Backyard

Age 2: Skipped this year because the last thing you want to celebrate is your kid turning two

Age 3: This cute gerbil tube place where the kids are locked inside clear tubes so the moms can sit and chat without interruption

Age 4: I can't remember

Age 5: The bounce house place (the first year she got to choose it herself)

So about six months before her sixth birthday (because that's how early you have to book shit), I had the dreaded conversation.

ME: Hey, Zoey, what kind of birthday party do you want this year?

ZOEY: A bounce house party.

ME: Or what about a princess party? Or a pirate party? Or a cooking party? Or a yoga party? Or a mini-golf party? Or an ice-skating party? Or a roller-skating party? Or a costume party? Or a Lego party? Or a painting party? Or a Build-A-Bear party? Or a nature place party? Or a cake decorating party? Or a pizza party? Or a superhero party? Or pretty much any other party you can think of in the whole entire world because I don't want to have ANOTHER F'ing bounce house party like we had last year?

ZOEY: No, I want a bounce house party.

Really? SERIOUSLY?!! I mean (a) it's expensive as shit, and (b) I have a heart attack every five seconds while I watch kids almost break their necks and stomp on each other's heads and WTF am I going to say to little Timmy's mom when she comes to pick him up?

ME: Thanks for coming, Timmy!! Don't forget to grab a party favor from the table and your brains from the bounce house where that big kid jumped on your head.

Anyways, I say no to my kids alllllll the time. Like seriously, one day I counted to see how many times I say no in a day and I lost count after 147. I wish I were kidding. But birthdays are like super important to kids, so I pretty much never say no.

ZOEY: Can I get my nails painted on my birthday?

ME: Sure.

ZOEY: Can I go to McDonald's on my birthday?

ME: We can do that.

ZOEY: Can I get a dog on my birthday?

ME: A stuffed one.

ZOEY: Can you call me Princess Zoey on my birthday?

ME: If that's what you want.

ZOEY: I want that.

ME: Sure thing, Your Highness.

So when it comes to her choosing the birthday party location, I always say yes. Correction: So far I've always said yes. Maybe not this year. Because last year she asked for the bounce house place and here's how it went down.

ZOEY: We're here, we're here!! It's my birthday party!!!

BOUNCE HOUSE LADY: Okay, Mom, just sign this waiver form and we can get started.

Hmmm, lemme read it first:

Please sign this to indicate that there is absolutely no way you can ever sue our asses, no matter WTF happens. Because here's some of the shit that might happen here: Your kid might get bruised, break a limb, break a neck, get smothered in a bounce house that deflates, or someone might jump on her head and her head might pop open like a Cadbury Creme Egg and all the filling might pour out. Oh yeah, and she might die.

ME: So lemme get this straight before I sign this waiver. If you guys pour baby oil all over the bounce houses and a kid slips and falls and dies, I can't sue you?

HER: *(super smiley)* That's right. Just sign it.

ME: Wait, what if you guys don't pay your electric bill and the lights go out and all the kids are trapped inside the collapsing bounce houses—

HER: *(perma-grin)* You can't do a thing. Just sign it.

ME: But what if—

HER: *(through a gritted smile)* Sign the motherfucking document, lady.

ME: Well, that seems fair. Do you have a pen?

And then one by one the parents all show up and sign their kids' lives away and drop them off so they can escape as quickly as possible to go run some random errand because there's not enough time to run to the grocery store because it's too long to leave your cold shit in the car but too short to go to the store you really need to go to because these bounce house places are always located in these weird industrial parks. Grrrrr.

Wheeeeeeee!!! They're bouncing!!!!! And their faces are getting super red and sweaty and they're running around like maniacs and, awwww shit, here comes another party. I totally forgot we might not be the only people in here. Yup, there's another birthday party going on at the same time, and these kids are older and they're all boys and they look like they're sumo wrestlers and they're mowing down our kids like giant John Deere tractors. Like there's this one man-child who looks like the dude who does a cannonball into a pool and literally all the water splashes out. Only in this scenario, the pool is a bounce house and the water is the kids from our party and when he jumps into the house all our kids fly out and land on their heads and break their necks and pretty much die. Wheeee, this is fun!!!

ZOEY: Mommmmmmmmm!!!!!!

I see Zoey running toward me and she has a look of terror on her face and I wonder if someone has died and, holy shit, is that blood dripping from her hair? OMG yes, something red is dripping from her hair. OMG OMG OMG.

ME: *(totally panicked and not cool and collected like I should be)* Zoey, what happened?!!!

ZOEY: Jasmine threw up in the bounce house!!!

And yup, now I can see that it is not in fact blood, it is red vomit and it is all in her hair and on her shirt and there are kids running around with red vomit all over them now. Because even if YOU don't serve the cake until after the bouncing part, that doesn't mean someone else in your kid's class didn't have a party earlier that day and serve cake with red frosting and pizza with red sauce like an hour before this party. Awesome. And I stand there wondering WTF to do and then I come up with a brilliant plan.

ME: TIME FOR CAKKKKE!!!!!!!!!!!!!!

And it looks like someone just fired the starter pistol at the marathon and kids of all sizes come running toward me at full speed, including all the sumo wrestlers, so I try to fix my mistake.

ME: Only for Zoey's party!!!!!!

Which is the stupidest thing I could yell because then all the sumo wrestlers do a one-eighty and start running in the other direction back to the bounce houses against the flow of traffic and there are collisions everywhere.

Bam! Bam! Bam! Bam! Bam!!!!

EVERY KID IN THE PLACE: Wahhhhhhhhhhhhh!!!!!!

And it looks like a scene after a bomb went off because people are lying all over the ground crying with red stains all over them.

Fifteen minutes later, the kids from Zoey's party are all sitting in complete silence wolfing down cake and you would never know anything bad just happened except for the pungent smell of puke that fills the room.

So this year, when Zoey asks me to have another bounce house party, I'm a total a-hole and I say no this time.

ME: No.

ZOEY: Please.

ME: No.

ZOEY: Pleeeeease.

ME: Nooooo. Ask again and you won't get a party at all.

ZOEY: *(silence)*

ME: How about a nice tea party?

ZOEY: Fiiiine.

End of story.

Oooooh, I just spent like 9,000 minutes on Pinterest looking at allllllll the adorable goodie bags I can do for my kid's birthday party!! And at the end of it, all I could think was that if I had just gone to the Dollar Store in the first place, this would be done by now.

You Want to Watch My Child?
BWHAHAHAHAHAHA!!
Oh Wait, You're Serious

YOU KNOW THOSE TOTALLY KICKASS MOMS WHO homeschool (no F'ing idea if that's one word or two) their kiddos and love being with them 25 hours a day? Yeah, I'm basically the opposite of that. Like right now while I'm writing this, my rugrats are at home because school was canceled after a blizzard last night and while they're shouting, "YAYYYYYYY, SCHOOL IS CANCELED!!!!!," I'm shouting a bunch of four-letter words into my pillow. Why? Because yes, I love being a mom, but I also lovvvvve being a mom who gets away from her kids sometimes. And by sometimes I mean for many hours every day when the kids are at school or camp or with their grandparents, a babysitter, or some random stranger who looks nice enough. Absence makes the heart grow fonder. And makes me not want to pop a little yellow pill or down a whole bottle of pills and check myself into the loony bin.

A letter to my kids' teachers

Dear Mr. or Ms. Badass,

Yeah, I know that's not really your name, but I'm calling you that. Because you, my friend, are amazing. Wait, that doesn't do your amazingness justice. You are SOOO F'ING AMAAAAAZING-GGGGG!!!!!!

Yeah, I know I probably shouldn't curse to my kids' teachers, so give me a detention or suspend me or whatever you want to do about it, but I'm done pussyfooting around. I mean I run into you at school or in the carpool line and I'm all tongue-tied like a lovestruck pubescent boy and you probably think I don't have vocal cords or something, but I actually do. I'm just a mom who is speechless with gratitude.

I mean let's just talk about what you do for a minute. You watch other people's crotchfruit alllllllll day long. Yeah, like WE had sex, WE got knocked up, and WE brought some little a-holes into this world, but YOU take care of them for more hours in the day than WE do. Seriously, I just did the math. Unless you're Michelle Duggar, taking care of TWENTY little kids all day is pretty much akin to Chinese water torture, only instead of drops of water dripping on your face over and over again until your fore-head looks like a donut, you're bombarded with snot and boogers and lice and drool and annoying questions, and if their fingers aren't up their nose to the second knuckle, then their hands are up their shorts doing God knows what to some other orifice. And even after all that, you still love the little boogersnots and take care of them better than their own parents do half the time.

Like when Zoey comes down the stairs in the morning wearing polka-dot pants with striped legwarmers with a furry vest over a red silk kimono, here's what goes through my head: WTF are you wearing? But here's what you say: "Wow, look at that kid's fierce independence." And either you truly believe it or you're such a good actor YOU should be giving Jack Nicholson acting lessons.

And speaking of the arts, you tell me all about this amazing picture Holden drew at the art table and how it's so awesome and how I should definitely frame it and you are so full of praise you clearly think my kiddo is a future Picasso. And then he takes it out of his folder to show me and it's a piece of paper with a line on it—like it looks like he accidentally hit a piece of paper with a crayon. Like you could give a starfish a crayon and he would do the same thing. But you really, truly, genuinely think it's awesome.

And then Holden has to put the drawing back into his folder and the folder back into his backpack and you stand there watch-

ing and watching and watching like you have allllllll afternoon and he can take as much time as he needs to get it in there, while in my head I'm screaming, "Oh, for the love of Gawdddd, just shove the F'ing folder into the F'ing backpack so we can leave already!!!!" And then when he finally finishes, you're like, "Good job, buddy. See you tomorrow." And I'm like, "It is tomorrow. That's how long we've been standing here waiting for him." Anyways, you . . . . . . are . . . . . . so . . . . . . patient . . . . . . it . . . . . . never . . . . . . ceases . . . . . . to . . . . . . amaze . . . . . . me.

But I guess you have to be when you're constantly waiting for twenty kids to go to the potty and wash their hands and eat their snacks and put their jackets on and put their backpacks away, etc., etc., etc. It's a miracle you have time to teach them anything. And yet, every day they come home and they've learned something new about math or reading or Modigliani or ~~ovapurous oviporus~~ oviparous animals (I still don't know WTF that is).

So thank you. Thank you for loving my children. Thank you for thinking they're awesome. Thank you for dealing with the shit that comes out of their orifices, literally and figuratively. Thank you for doing it all for way too little compensation. Thank you for making them smarter. Thank you for making them smarter than me. (Than I? Shit, I don't know which one's right.) Thank you for knowing shit like that so you can teach it to them because if it were up to me, they'd be screwed.

> *Love and kisses,*
> *A mom who worships the ground you walk on*

ME: *What'd you do at school today?*

ZOEY: *Nothing.*

ME: *Who'd you play with?*

ZOEY: *No one.*

ME: *Did you read any books?*

ZOEY: *I can't remember.*

ME: *Are you F'ing kidding me?*

ZOEY: *I don't know.*

Halle-F'ing-lujah, both kids are finally in school

ME: Who's excited for school?!!

HOLDEN: Me!!

ME: Who's a big boy and going to school just like his sister?!

HOLDEN: Me!!

ME: We're almost there. Who can't wait?!!!

HOLDEN: Meeeee!!!!

(three minutes later)

HOLDEN: Nooooooo!!!!!! Wahhhhhh!!! Don't leave me!!!! You're the worst mommy everrrrr!!!!!

I desperately try to lower my screaming child to the ground, but it's pretty much impossible because his hands are superglued around my neck and every time I try, his legs wrap around me in a vise grip and he won't stand up and we're basically in a mosh pit of lululemon-wearing stick figures who are smothering their kiddos with air kisses and judging me for being the shittiest mom ever.

Finally, the teacher comes out of the classroom to "help."

TEACHER: Awwww, who's this little guy?

ME: This is the devil's spawn.

I don't really say that out loud because it's the beginning of the school year so I'm still trying to make the teachers think that I'm a nice, normal person.

ME: This is Holden.

TEACHER: Awwwww, hi Holden. Wanna come with me, sweetie?

You're so observant. He definitely wants to come with you. NOT. Yo lady, pry his F'ing nails out of my humerus bone and drag him into your classroom because that is the only way this is gonna happen.

TEACHER: *(whispers)* If we need to, we can always put a chair in the room and you can transition out of there more slowly.

I've got three little words for you:
F that shit.
There is no way I am sitting in a chair in the classroom. Because (a) that's like ripping the Band-Aid off slowwwwwwwwly over weeks of excruciating pain. And (b) whenever I sit in one of

those little preschool chairs, my ass spills over the sides and looks extra gigantic.

ME: Holden, stop crying and listen to me. Mommy will come back to get you in two hours. I promise.

HOLDEN: I *(air suck)* don't *(air suck)* want *(air suck)* you *(air suck)* to leave *(air suck)* meeee.

TEACHER: What if Mommy stays in the building? Would that be better?

Ugghh, seriously? I totally wanted to go shopping.

HOLDEN: I *(air suck)* want *(air suck)* her *(air suck)* to *(air suck)* stayyy *(air suck)*.

TEACHER: Mommy . . .

Okay, let's just pause for a moment here because I have a question for the teacher. Here's what I want to know. Did you come out of my vagina? 'Cause I'm pretty sure I would remember a squat redheaded lady with purple glasses coming out of my hooha, and that doesn't ring a bell. Which means that I am not *Mommy*. You can call me Mrs. Alpert. You can call me Karen. You can call me Holden's Mommy. You can call me pretty much anything you want, but unless you came out of my vagina, you may not call me *Mommy*. But of course I don't say this out loud.

TEACHER: Mommy, there is a teachers' lounge down the hall where some of the other mommies are waiting. How does that sound?

Shitty.

ME: Fine.

By this point Holden is so tired that I'm able to peel his fingers off my skin and lower him to the ground. Of course, he's still trying to fight gravity and his legs are up, so I place him on his tush.

ME: *(trying to be chipper)* You're gonna have so much fun, buddy! I'll be back in a little while!!

Whatever you do, do NOT turn around and look at him. Seriously, don't do it. Do not look. But of course, I can't help it and I turn my head and our eyes meet and he breaks into hysterical cries. Awww shit. Just keep walking. I walk down the hall looking for the teachers' lounge, and after opening like four wrong doors, I finally find it. It's filled with all those lululemon ladies who look at me with "pity eyes" the moment I walk in.

ONE OF THEM: Did he stop crying?

ANOTHER ONE: Is he okay?

AND ANOTHER: We felt sooooo bad for you.

Because my kid is crying or because my pants have a boring old Champion logo on them?

ME: Thanks. He'll be fine.

ONE OF THEM: Oh, I couldn't have left. You're so brave *(translation: mean)*.

ANOTHER ONE OF THEM: I totally thought *mine* would be the one to cry today. I was so nervous, I could barely sleep last night until I popped an Ambien.

Oh yeah, I couldn't sleep last night either. Because I was SOOOOO F'ing excited!!!! You GET to drop your kid off at a place two times a week where trained professionals will take care of your rugrat while you GET to go off all alone and get shit done. Why on earth would you be nervous? And that's when the lightbulb goes off over my head. Ohhh, these are FIRST-TIME moms!! That explains it. This was *me* three years ago. Minus the fancy yoga pants. Plus some really bad nervous poops.

ME: It's not a big deal. He's my second child.

IN UNISON: Ahhhhhhhh.

And that's when some random lady from the school pops her head into the doorway.

RANDOM LADY: Just here to give a little update to you ladies. All of the kids are doing great!

They all sigh with relief.

RANDOM LADY: Except for Holden. He's still adjusting.

ME: Okay.

RANDOM LADY: But you don't have to worry, he's going to do just fine.

ME: I know.

RANDOM LADY: Please don't worry.

ME: I'm not. Really.

And all the first-time preschool moms look at me with pity to see if I'm upset and I'm like, "Seriously guys, I am fiiiiine. This is my second child!!"

(Insert lots of boring talk about exercise classes and where do people know each other from and other shit I stop listening to until Mrs. Random Update Lady pops in again.)

RANDOM LADY: They're all doing art right now and loving it!!

Oh good!

RANDOM LADY: Except for Holden. He's still getting used to the classroom.

Go figure. The woman next to me puts her hand on my knee.

WOMAN: It's okay.

Uhhh, yeah, I know it's okay because a little crying never hurt a child. Do I feel bad for him? Sure. Do I feel bad for myself? A little. But I've done this before. I mean not *exactly* this because the first time I took Zoey to school she was pretty much shooting me the bird with both hands over her head as she marched away, but it's not like she hasn't cried about other shit. So yeah, been there, done that.

Anyways, this went on for the rest of the two hours and then it was time to go pick them up. Actually, it was still five minutes early but one eager beaver jumped up to go be first in the pickup line so everyone followed. And guess who was the first kid to come out of the classroom with a giant, humongous smile across his face? Someone else's kid. Mine came out second with a giant frown and was like, thank F'ing God my mom is here.

ME: Good job today, buddy!

TEACHER: I think he got a *little* better.

No, he didn't.

TEACHER: And he used the potty after snack.

ME: Great.

ONE OF THE OTHER MOMS: He's potty trained?

ME: Yes.

ANOTHER ONE: Does he wear Pull-Ups?

ME: No.

AND ANOTHER: Really?

ME: Really.

AND ANOTHER: That's *amazing*.

And there you go. Win.

Oh, wait, what's that I smell? Did one of your little butt-munches make a poopie in his diaper? I wonder which mom I should look at with pity?

A. The mom in the tennis skirt

B. The mom with the Mercedes baseball cap

C. None of them

FYI, the correct answer is "C." Your kid still poops in his pants and my kid cries at drop-off. They'll both get over it. One day you'll be dropping your kid off at college and he won't be wearing diapers and I'll be dropping my kid off at college and he won't be freaking out and clinging to me. Actually, quite the opposite.

ME: Wahhhhhhhh!!! Nooooooo!! Don't leave meeeeee!!!!!

HOLDEN: Mom, please let go of me. This is so embarrassing.

ME: *Zoey, what'd you do in school today?*

ZOEY: *We talked about Martin Loser King.*

ME: *Who?*

ZOEY: *Martin Loser King.*

ME: *LUTHER. Martin LUTHER King.*

I'm really glad I turned off the radio so we could have this little chat.

What NOT to F'ing do when you're taking care of your grandkids

Dear Granny, Grampy, Nana, and Pop Pop,

Thank you sooooo much for taking care of the kids next week so the hubby and I can go away for the first time in years. I know I'm just supposed to be appreciative, so lemme tell you a little something that I would appreciate. I would appreciate coming back to the same kids we left behind. 'Cause in the past when we've left them with you for just one evening, we come back and I literally can't tell where their buttholes are because both kids have turned into the most gigantic assholes I've ever seen. I know you think that taking care of your grandpoopers is your chance to relive the glory days, but these are not YOUR kids. These are OUR kids. And if they act more a-holey than usual when we return, then going on vacation has actually made life more stressful, which means I just paid a shitload of money for my life to get worse.

So here you go, my little geriatric friends. This is a list of shit NOT to do while we are gone:

1. *Please do not constantly stuff my kids with candy. For some reason whenever I walk out of the room you suddenly turn into a Mexican piñata maker and stuff my kids silly with candy like they're hollow papier-mâché donkeys. If we get back and the kids are high on Pixy Stix and Pop Rocks, I'm putting a blindfold on, grabbing a stick, and beating the crap out of the nearest grandparent.*

2. *Please do not keep the TV on constantly in the background. (a) Since you have the volume turned up to 99, it is not in the background, and (b) if my kids watch TV for a week straight they will literally turn into zombies and suck your brains out. Karma.*

3. *Speaking of television, please do not let them watch shows other than the ones that are on the "approved" list. Because if they get hooked on* Caillou *or* Max & Ruby *or some other annoying show, I am going on Pinterest and I'm learning how to make thongs out of dental floss and then I am going into your closet and secretly replacing all your granny panties.*

4. *Seat belts, car seats, bike helmets, pill bottles, sunscreen, plastic bags, sharp objects, EpiPens, etc., etc., etc. These things are not debatable. Yeah, I know you think you're joking when you say it's a miracle your own kids are alive today, but I'm dead serious when I answer, "Yes, it is."*

5. *Please do not send my kids out to play at 9 a.m. and call them back in for dinner at 5 p.m. like it's the good ol' days. Because playing with the neighbors all day is super fun until you find out the neighbor is a sixty-year-old man with a Polaroid camera, an anonymous Instagram account, and more duct tape than Home Depot.*

6. *Bedtime is not two hours AFTER bedtime. And two minutes BEFORE bedtime is not a good time to start watching a movie or make chocolate sundaes or go outside to play. Just because I'm adjusting to a different time zone doesn't mean they have to too.*

7. *Please do not let them skip school or their activities while we are gone. I know you think it's okay because it's just a special treat, but guess what? Not learning how to do math or read is not a special treat. And neither is being a homeless person who lives under a bridge because you can't get a job because you don't know how to do math or read.*

8. *Okay, here's some shit I don't want to find when I get back to my house: whistles, horns, xylophones, cowbells, finger paints, permanent markers, window markers, bath crayons, fake weapons, real weapons, lawn ornaments, new pets, or*

other annoying shit that wasn't in my house when I left. If you desperately feel the need to buy them something, buy them underwear. Or buy them jewelry to give to me.

9. *When I hand you the list of emergency phone numbers, please don't poo-poo me and toss them aside. I'm not questioning your ability to handle an emergency. I'm questioning your ability to know the pediatrician's phone number off the top of your head when my kid pokes his eyeball out with the scissors you gave him.*

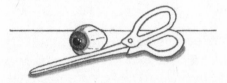

10. *If one of the kids misses us, do not tell them we cannot bother Mommy and Daddy on vacation. Put the iPad in their hands and let them Skype us. Please take note that I did not say, "You should Skype us." I said, "Let THEM Skype us." Because you're absolutely right, YOU don't want to bother us on vacation.*

That's it. Have an awesome time! And just remember, one day in the not too distant future, we will be choosing where you live.

Love and kisses,
THE parents

Sometimes I feel a little guilty that my kids never learn very much at home, until I remember, wait a sec, yes they do. I teach them new vocabulary words every day!

The really serious chapter about something that sucks big-time

DOO DOO DOO DOO DOOOOOO, driving home from the library where I just dropped off eleven books that were just a few days late and one book that was due seventeen weeks ago but I didn't know about it until the library called me to ask me where the F it was so I had to search around the house like a maniac and finally found it under Holden's mattress. WTF, kid, it's a book about ferrets, not a *Playboy*.

Hmmm, maybe I'll take a longer route home. You know, because it's the scenic route. Bwhahahahaha. There is no such thing as the scenic route in our town. Ohhhh, look at the beautiful sunset over DSW. Seriously, that's as pretty as it gets. Not that I haven't bought some seriously beautiful shoes there.

Anyways, no, there is another reason I'm deciding to take the longer route home, but I'm embarrassed to tell you. I'm a little scared you're gonna think I'm a nutjob. Not that you don't already think that, but even more of a nutjob. Okay, wait, before I explain why I take the longer route home and embarrass myself, here's the backstory.

So a few years ago, I was at a playdate and my friend and I had this conversation.

BELLE: Did you hear about the boy in Springfield?

ME: No.

BELLE: At the hot dog place?

ME: Do I want to hear?

Nope, no, I do not want to hear. Because even though I'm sitting there praying she says something like, "He found a finger in his French fries" or "He got kicked out of the restaurant for pooping on the table," I'm pretty sure from the tone of her voice that this is going to be worse. Much worse.

BELLE: He choked on a hot dog.

ME: *(silence)*

BELLE: And died.

A million questions go through my head. Where were his parents? Had they cut the hot dog in half? Were the kids sitting at a different table and no one noticed? Did they just find him slumped over and then realize? Did they notice while it was happening and try to do the Heimlich? Did they sweep his mouth with their finger and push the hot dog farther into his throat? Did the mother scream? Did the whole restaurant notice this was going on? Was the boy afraid? Oh my God, how awful.

And for years, I've been thinking about it. I mean not incessantly every single day, but pretty much every time I cut a hot dog in half for my kiddos, I think about that boy and his poor, poor family.

Before I had kids, this kind of story would spontaneously combust in my mind a few minutes after I heard it, but nowadays, there's a little section of my brain where these stories stack up and haunt me. The boy who went to the public pool with his camp and drowned. The girl who was crushed by the bookshelf that fell on her. The two-year-old who went down for a nap and didn't wake up. I mean this kind of shit doesn't happen every day, but it gets talked about so much, you would think it's not all that rare.

And then I heard the worst one of all. I flipped on my television one day (thank God the kids weren't around) and there it was. Newtown. Oh my God. Not OMG because this is way too serious for an acronym. Oh my God, oh my God, OH MY GOD. As I watched the news unfold, my heart broke into a thousand pieces for those families. I would say *I can't imagine,* but I can. I imagine it all the time. What that scene must have looked like with all those adorable little first graders. The thought of waiting for your kid to come out of the school, and waiting. And waiting.

Hold on a sec, I need to grab a tissue. Seriously, it is impossible for me to think about Newtown without getting teary-eyed.

And here's the thing. It's turned me into a crazy person. I mean the hot dog story made me start cutting my kids' hot dogs down the center, and the bookshelf kid made me bolt my one and only bookshelf to the wall even though it's in the guest room where the kids never go, and the two-year-old who never woke up made me watch the video monitor a little closer, but the Newtown story has literally made me act like a crazy person. It's what makes me take the longer route home from the library. Not every day, but once in a while. Why?

Because the longer route means I can drive by my daughter's school.

About a block away, I start looking for flashing lights. Are there any cop cars or fire engines? Nope, the school looks peaceful from the outside. But Newtown probably looked peaceful from the outside too. At least until everyone started running out. And then I'm closer to the school and I see a man going in. Is he a workman or a teacher or is he some messed-up kind of psychopath who has two guns under his coat that he's going to whip out when he gets to the office? My mind starts to go to a bad place, but then I see that he's just a sandwich delivery guy. Phew. But I hate that I even think this way. It cannot be normal.

And sometimes when Zoey's jumping out of the car in the morning, I make her jump back in to give me a kiss or I'm careful to yell, "I love you!!" even though three minutes earlier I was going ballistic on her because she wouldn't put her seat belt on. I make sure that last moment when I say good-bye for the day is extra loving. Because what if it's the last time?

I can't be totally crazy because I'm not the only one who's thinking about the worst-case scenario. One day earlier this year, Zoey came home from school and told me they practiced a lockdown drill, you know, in case a skunk got into the building. That's what they told the kids since they're only kindergarteners and how can they tell a bunch of kindergarteners that it's actually because a crazy man went into a school in Newtown and sprayed all the first graders with bullets and turned all those sweet little babies into angels. No, we can't tell kindergarteners that.

I guess I'm a grown-up so I can handle it. But not really.

(Zoey and I both just farted at the same time)

ZOEY: *Jinx fart.*

Who the hell knew that if two people fart at the same time,
it's a jinx fart? My kindergartener might not know how
to read yet, but she's learned what a jinx fart is at school.
Awesome.

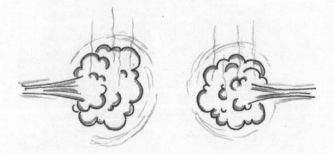

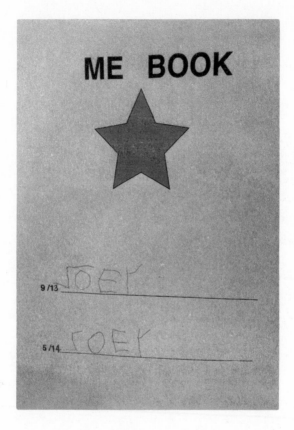

Dear Zoey's school,
I want my money back.

And for Dinner
I Gave My Kids an
EATING DISORDER

YEAH, MY KID USED TO EAT BROCCOLI. BACK when she was in my womb and got her food via umbilical cord. And then she was born and decided that anything green is poisonous and will make her die instantly. Well, I assume that's what she thinks because if I put it on her plate she screams and cries like someone is chasing her with a hatchet. So whatta I do? I beg and plead and bribe her to try it and it's just like that old TV show *Fear Factor*, where you're supposed to eat cockroach eyeballs or lizard gizzards, only my kid doesn't walk away with $50,000. She walks away with nine eating disorders. Anyways, I don't know how some parents get their kids to eat all kinds of healthy shit. Like when I go out to eat sushi, there's always a table with a family sitting next to us and the kiddos are wolfing down baby octopus with sea urchin and I totally want to go over and ask the mom how she does it. You know, after I punch her because I kinda sorta hate her a little.

Every. F'ing. Night.

ZOEY: Can I have dessert?

ME: You haven't touched your carrots.

ZOEY: Can I have dessert if I eat them?

ME: This isn't about dessert. This is about putting healthy things in our bodies.

ZOEY: But how many do I have to eat to get dessert?

ME: It's not about how many. Just eat *some* of them.

ZOEY: But how many?!!

ME: Why don't you start with one?

ZOEY: Will that be enough to get dessert?

ME: We might not have dessert tonight.

ZOEY: If I eat my carrots can I have dessert?

ME: AGGGGHHHH, stop saying the word *dessert* and just eat some!!!!!!

ZOEY: They're cold.

ME: No shit, Sherlock. Because we've been sitting here for like 6,000 hours talking about dessert.

ZOEY: They're freeeeezing.

ME: Fine, I'll nuke them.

ZOEY: Now they're too hot.

ME: Just wait a minute. They'll cool down.

ZOEY: Then they'll be too cold.

ME: I'll bet they're fine now.

ZOEY: What are we having for dessert?

ME: I don't know.

ZOEY: Can I have ice cream for dessert?

ME: If you eat your carrots.

ZOEY: But how many?

ME: Oh my gawwwwd, how many times are you going to ask me that?!!!!

ZOEY: How many? How many? How many? How many?

ME: Fine, three.

ZOEY: Three bites?

ME: Three carrots.

ZOEY: Ugggh, that is SO many.

ME: Fine, don't eat any.

ZOEY: But then I can't have dessert.

ME: It's not about that.

(She puts a carrot to her mouth and takes the most minuscule bite you've ever seen, like Barbie would take a bigger bite than that.)

ME: See? It's good.

ZOEY: Huuaggghh, huuagggh, huaaggghh *(in case you can't tell, this is the sound dogs make before they throw up)*.

ME: It's not that bad, Zoey.

Barrrrrrffffff. Is it wrong that the first thing that goes through my head is not "Are you okay?" It's happiness that the throw-up all lands on her plate.

ZOEY: Now can I have dessert?

ME: Fine, I give up.

(I look in the freezer.)

ME: We're out of ice cream.

ZOEY: That's not fair!!!! You said I could have ice cream if I tried a carrot.

ME: I did not say that. And you didn't eat one.

ZOEY: I did!

ME: Fine, you can have as much ice cream as the carrot you ate.

(I take out a bowl and put it down in front of her, empty.)

ZOEY: Can I get more if I eat more carrots?

ME: *(sigh)* Sure.

(I put some more carrots on a new plate in front of her.)

ZOEY: How many do I have to eat?

WTF?

Seriously, if I don't move that one damn pea before I put it down in front of her, the entire meal will be deemed inedible.

How to properly
ruin a friend's BBQ

OKAY, HERE'S THE THING. WHEN I go to a restaurant and I bring food for my kids, I know I'm a jackass. Which is why I don't need you, Muffy McPerfectpants, to keep staring at me like I'm a jackass. I already know!!! Yes, I see your kiddo ordering off the menu. Yes, I see her wolfing down a spinach salad and gnawing away on a rack of ribs and using chopsticks. And not in the fake kinda way my kids use them by stabbing their chicken nuggets and then eating them like lollipops. And if you think I'm just being jealous, you are 2,000% right. I would KILL to have a child who eats food like a normal human being and doesn't act like I'm trying to feed her goat scrotum when I put a sandwich down in front of her.

Anyways, having picky eaters sucks ass. Like here's the kind of shit that happens:

FRIEND: We're having people over for a BBQ Sunday night. Do you guys want to come?

ME: DO I?!!!!! You're like the coolest mom ever and I can't believe you're inviting me over!!!

Of course, I don't really say that out loud because I don't want to seem too eager.

(what I really say)

ME: Lemme check my calendar.

It's all empty, just one white square after another.

ME: Hmmm, sure, I can move things around to make that work.

FRIEND: Great! Do your kids like hot dogs?

ME: Umm, no, but don't worry, I can bring food for them.

FRIEND: What about chicken?

ME: No, but seriously, I'll just bring something.

FRIEND: Hamburgers?

ME: No.

FRIEND: Turkey burgers?

ME: No.

FRIEND: Corn?

ME: Okay, seriously, I'll bring something for them. I do it all the time.

FRIEND: Okay.

And then the day of the BBQ arrives and even though we've been waiting around all afternoon counting down the minutes, for some reason when it's finally time to leave our house we're running late and I turn into Cujo and have to yell at my kids to get their shoes on and then when they finally do Holden says he has to poop, and since Holden's poops smell like an old man took a dump and then died on the toilet, we go back inside to do it in our own home because otherwise we'd have to do it at my new friend's house and I'd have to go into the bathroom with Holden and my new friend would never believe a smell that bad could come from a little boy's tush and she would totally think it was me who made the paint peel off her bathroom walls. But I digress. And holy shit, that might be the longest sentence I've ever written in my entire life.

Anyways, the BBQ is so much fun. The kids get to bounce in a bounce house, the dads get to man the grill, and the moms get to suck down margaritas and actually finish complete sentences for a change. And then it's time for dinner.

Yummmmm, it looks sooooo deeelicious, but it'll be at least twenty minutes before the moms get to eat anything because setting up the kids with food takes forevvvver.

HOSTESS TO HER KID: Here you go, sweetie pie, a burger and a salad.

Holy shit, her kid eats salad?!!!

ANOTHER MOM TO HER KID: How did you already finish your veggies? You are a total veggie-aholic.

OMG, I am literally drooling with jealousy.

ANOTHER MOM: See? I told you you'd like hummus, honey.

And then there's me. Unwrapping my embarrassing tinfoil package of chicken nuggets and veggie straws (made of real veggies but I'm pretty sure the way they make them is by taking real vegetables and sucking any redeeming qualities out of them) as quietly as possible so no one notices the shitty processed food I brought for my kids to eat. It's like every single crinkle in the tinfoil makes the loudest noise you can imagine, and every child within a two-block radius hears me and sees what I'm doing.

HOSTESS'S KIDDO: Mommy, can I have chicken nuggets?

ANOTHER KIDDO: Yeah, I want chicken nuggies!

OTHER KID: Me too!

And they push their plates away and start banging on the table.

KIDS EVERYWHERE AROUND THE WORLD: We want nuggets! We want nuggets! We want nuggets!

Awwwwww shit, busted. And guess who didn't bring extra chicken nuggets for all the other kids? Yup, I'm that asshole. The asshole who carefully counted out ten chicken nuggets and was too stoopid to pack more for the other kids, just in case.

HOSTESS: No, Ariel, eat your hamburger.

OTHER MOM: The nuggets are only for kids with allergies, honey.

Uhhhh, yeahhhh, my kids have allergies, that's it. Shit, I totally should have just lied and said that in the first place. But it's too late. Plates are being thrown, kids are freaking out, and the moms are desperately pleading with their kids to eat the regular BBQ food.

KID: Nooooo, I HATE veggies!! I want nuggets!

ANOTHER KID: Wahhhhhh, I don't want regeeler chicken!!! I want veggie straws!

KID: It's not fair!! I want veggie straws and I want them NOWWWW!!!!

And since I don't want to be an even bigger asshole, I take some veggie straws off my kids' plates, and divide them up so every kid has a few, which seriously pisses off Zoey and Holden.

ZOEY: Nooooooo!!! Those are mine!!!!

HOLDEN: Wahhhhhhh!!! Give me back my veggie straws!!

And Holden throws himself across the table to grab his veggie straws back and he ends up knocking three plates off the table including Zoey's. And the family dog who's been patiently watching the whole scene sees his cue and bolts over and catches Zoey's plate in midair like a Frisbee and wolfs down like every single chicken nugget and veggie straw in one gigantic gulp and holy crap do the kids go ballistic now.

RUGRAT: Nooooo, Bailey!!!

KIDDO: It was all the chicken nuggets we had!!!!

ZOEY: Wahhhhh!!!! What am I going to eat nowwww?!!!!

Hmmm, I don't know, what on earth could you eat now? Mayyybe, oh, here's an idea, how about a huge, juicy, delicious hamburger? I put it down on her plate.

ZOEY: AGGGHHHH, NOOO, GET IT OFF!! GET IT OFFFF!!!

HOSTESS: Who wants dessert?!

And the scene literally goes from a mess of snot and tears to a scene of total jubilation.

KIDS: Ice cream! Ice cream! Ice cream! Ice cream!

And just like that, it's the best BBQ ever and the rest of the evening is totally awesome, which pretty much sucks donkey butt because I'm 200% sure we are never going to be invited back there again. Ever.

And that, my friends, is what it's like to have picky eaters. So believe me, if there was anything I could do to make my kids like regular food and eat like normal human beings, I would do it.

HOLDEN: *Hey, Nemo is on my cup!*

ME: *Yup.*

HOLDEN: *But I want two Nemos.*

ME: *Well, there's only one.*

HOLDEN: *But I want TWO!*

ME: *Fine. Here's Nemo.*

I point to Nemo on his cup.

Then I spin the cup ALL the way around.

ME: *And here's another Nemo.*

HOLDEN: *Yay, two Nemos!*

Dear parents who don't think it's fair to ban nuts from school

Dear Parents at _____ School who don't think it's fair for the school to ban nut products,

So I just heard the story about your school and even though my kids don't go there, I still couldn't help but have an opinion. Now if you don't want to hear what I think, feel free to stop reading now. Seriously, stop reading 'cause you might not agree with what I say.

Okay, you're still with me. Here we go.

So lemme get this straight. There's this kid who's deathly allergic to nuts. Like it's so bad that if this kid sat down at a table where someone was eating nuts, he would die. As in dead. Gone. Forever. And the only way this kid can go to school is if the school bans EVERYONE from bringing nut products into the school.

And lemme make sure I understand where you're coming from. So you think it's YOUR kid's right to bring her favorite snack to school. You think if someone tells her she can't bring a PB&J to lunch that her freedom is being squashed.

Am I understanding all of this so far? I just want to make sure I have this straight.

Okay.

So are you ready for my opinion? Do you want to hear what I think? Stop being such a goddamn shartrag and grow the F up. I mean seriously? SERIOUSLY?!!! You think your kid's right to eat a stupid brownie with chopped nuts in it is more important than a kid's life? Your kid can still eat her crappy PB&J. She's just gonna have to wait a few extra hours until she gets home from school.

I'm sorry if it's inconvenient for you to have to think a little harder about what you pack in little Timmy's lunchbox. Think how F'ing hard it is for Allergy Boy's mom every damn day trying to figure out where he can and can't go, and what he can and can't eat. How awful it must be for her to send her kid off every day knowing she might not see him again if he accidentally touches the wrong table.

"But but but can't this kid get homeschooled?" you ask. Ummm, first of all, are you offering to homeschool him, because who the hell said his mom can do that? Duh, maybe she works like most parents do.

"Well, why should my love muffin have to stop bringing banana nut muffins to school because some other kid has allergies?"

I'll tell you why. It's called compassion. It's called putting yourself in another mother's shoes. It's called teaching your kid that maybe, just maybe, her desire to take peanut M&M's to school isn't quite as important as a boy's life.

Anyways, that's just my measly two cents. Take it or leave it. I'm off to the kitchen where I'm going to eat a scoop of peanut butter, because it's not gonna hurt anyone, because I'm at home.

Sincerely,
A mom who gives a crap about ALL kids,
not just my own

HUBBY: *I'm getting a milk shake.*

ME: *But the kids didn't eat enough to get one.*

HUBBY: *So? I did.*

ME: *Yeah, but if YOU get one, they're totally gonna want one too.*

HUBBY: *I'll just tell them no.*

ME: *Then they're gonna be whiny a-holes the whole way home and we're gonna have to listen to that shit.*

HUBBY: *Fine, I won't let them see it.*

ME: *Yeah, right. Like that'll work.*

I stand corrected. Thank God for winter hats!

Once upon a time there was a green bean

ME: Guys, don't forget to eat your green beans. You haven't taken a single bite.

ZOEY: Mommy, will you tell us how green beans are made?

ME: Well, they're not really made. They grow.

ZOEY: Nooooo, tell us the pretend way.

ME: Ohhh, the pretend way.

Ugggh, seriously? I am SOOOOO sick of telling these stupid pretend food stories. So once we went to this restaurant and the food was taking a long time to come out, and my kids were all, "Wahhhh, where's our fooood?" and I answered, "Well, it takes the chef a long time to go out and kill the pizzas," and then they were like, "Nuh-uhhh," and I was like, "Yuh-huhhh. The pizzas are born on a pizza farm and then they have to grow bigger and then when someone orders a pepperoni pizza, the chef has to go out to the field and find the right one and lasso it but the pizzas keep rolling away so it takes a while."

Anyways, my kids aren't idiots (except when they play a stupid game like "let's push each other on the stairs and see who gets hurt"), so they knew I was kidding but they lovvvvved my story. And now every time we're eating (THREE F'ing times a day), they're all, "Tell us how they make the pizzas," or "Tell us where they get the apples," or "Tell us where the macaroni and cheese comes from," and I have to use my brain a lot and come up with these silly stories.

At first, telling these stories was fun and funny and I enjoyed doing it, but now I'm like, aggghhhh, can't you just act like normal crotchmuffins and play with the salt and pepper shakers and leave me the hell alone? All I want to do is just eat my food in peace. Is that too much to ask?!! But fine, whatever, if it'll make you happy.

ZOEY: Pleeeease tell us the story about the green beans.

ME: Okay, fine, the story about the green beans.

I repeat her words because I'm stalling and trying to come up with a creative story I haven't told before.

ME: So the green beans grow in big fields on the bottom of the ocean.

ZOEY: So they're like seaweed?

ME: Kind of. But they're green beans. And they grow in these big patches until this ginormous purple octopus with eight arms comes along and he uses all his arms to give the green beans a huge hug and he picks them all at once and swims up to the surface to deliver the green beans to the fishermen and while he's swimming up with them, the green beans sing this song.

We are the green beans, the green beans of the sea,
We grow from the ocean floor, come and eat me . . .

And yes, I know it's like the stupidest song ever, but I'm making it up on the spot. Plus, while I'm singing it I'm actually thinking about which bottle of wine I'm going to open up tonight once the kiddos go to bed. Two more hours, two more hours, two more hours.

Anyways, the song goes on for a few more lines, and as soon as I'm done singing it, Zoey has a question.

ZOEY: Wait, are the green beans sad?

ME: Sad? No, why?

ZOEY: Because they're gonna get eaten.

 Awww shit, she totally took my story and spun it and now she's gonna refuse to eat her green beans because now they have feelings. Shit shit shit shit shit. You better fix this now.

ME: Oh nooooo. Not at all. The green beans *want* to get eaten.

ZOEY: They do?

ME: Yup, that's how they fulfill their life dream.

ZOEY: Really?

She looks doubtful.

ME: Really. That is *literally* why they are born. That is their life purpose. To get eaten. The only sad green beans are the ones that are still left on the plate.

Zoey looks down at the four sad green beans lying on her plate looking up at her. I mean no, they don't really have eyes, but you know, I'm personifying or whatever the F that's called.

And the next thing I know, she's gobbling up every green bean on her plate. By the last one, she's making a face like she can hardly take it anymore, but she finishes and looks satisfied.

And all the green beans lived happily ever after. Chewed up and slowly turning into poop. Except for Holden's. He took a bite of one (poor amputee green bean), but the other two were dumped into the trash can where they were sad forever and ever. Not really. Really they high-fived each other and had a big party because they avoided getting eaten, but don't tell my kids that.

The End.

HOLDEN: *Mommy, do you want some penis?*

I was about to say, "Ummm, no thank you," until I turned around and saw him holding the jar of peanuts from the pantry. Phew.

ME: *Yes, please.*

Conversations I've had
with my picky eaters

ME: Do you want oatmeal, cereal, eggs, or a bagel?

HOLDEN: I don't know. Give me choices.

•

ZOEY: How many bites do I have to eat to get dessert?

ME: 2,927,103. I'm assuming they're each gonna be the size of an atom.

•

ZOEY: Aggghhh, get it off, GET IT OFF!!!!!!! Hurry!!!!!! GET IT OFFFFF!!!

ME: Umm, excuse me, waitress, but can you remove the pickle from her plate?

•

ME: Muhahahahaha, I put spinach in your smoothie and you have no idea!!! But alas, I cannot brag about it or you'll never fall for it again. Sigh.

HOLDEN: Nooooo, you peeled it too much!!!

ME: No, I didn't, buddy. Look.

And I take out the tape measure and show him that the banana is 8 inches long and I peeled it to exactly 4 inches, precisely halfway, just the way he likes it.

•

ZOEY: It's not fair!!! Holden got more bread than me!!!!

ME: Yeah, but you got a hole in your bread and he didn't.

HOLDEN: Wahhh, I want a hole in my bread!! It's not fair!!!

•

ZOEY: Mommm, this milk tastes like cow udders.

ME: Ewwww, I can't even begin to imagine what cow udders taste like. Wait, yes, I can, and Zoey Lila Alpert, you are NOT allowed to think about that until you are much, much older.

Alllllllll the things my kids won't eat, even if they are literally starving to death

A bun if there are poppy seeds on it

Pasta if there is green shit on top

Hot dogs if there are lines on it from the grill

A bagel if it's toasted

A bagel if it's too cold

Any apple except for a Honeycrisp apple

Any apple if I accidentally leave a tiny piece of the peel on it

The stupid little carrots and celery in a can of chicken noodle soup

Any constructed food item—cheese and crackers, tacos, s'mores, they all have to be deconstructed

Fruit if it's green

The entire banana if there's a brown spot on it anywhere

The outside of the ravioli (so, yes, I peel that shit off)

Anything on their plate if there's one thing on their plate they don't like

A pea if it's wrinkly

A carrot if it's been cut in half

Food they like that's touching any food they don't like, like even though Zoey loves cantaloupe, she won't eat it if it's in a fruit salad touching honeydew

Guacamole if you can tell it was made with avocado

Marinara sauce if there are tomatoes in it (hmmm)

Chicken nuggets that aren't shaped like Mickey Mouse

Grilled cheese made with fancy cheese

Mac and cheese made with fancy cheese

Mac and cheese if there are bread crumbs on top (which means I have to eat the bread crumbs off, yayyy!)

A smoothie if they can detect any ingredient in it

Hot dogs without ketchup

French fries without ketchup

Chicken nuggets without ketchup

Their entire bowl of cereal if there's one of those little burnt pieces in there

Bread with crust on it

Seedless watermelon if there are any seeds in it

Applesauce that's in a bowl even though they'll happily suck it out of a pouch

Tater tots (which officially makes them insane)

Bacon if it's not crispy enough

Bacon if it's too burnt

Square pizza slices without a handle (crust)

Anything once they've tasted it and it's too hot

And like a shitload of other things, but I can't keep writing it all right now because I have to go make dinner. And by make dinner, I mean call Domino's. And God help us if we order half cheese, half pepperoni and one of the cheese pieces has a sliver of pepperoni on it and it ends up on one of my kids' plates. Holy crap, shit fest.

ZOEY: *Wow, Mommy, that building is soooo beautiful. What is it?*

ME: *Taco Bell.*

And when I've had way too much to drink, I feel exactly the same way, kiddo.

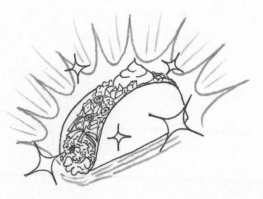

Here an Orifice,
THERE AN ORIFICE,
Everywhere an Orifice Orifice

I DON'T KNOW ABOUT YOU, BUT I SPEND CRAZY amounts of time in the bathroom with my little poop machines. Seriously, I just did the math and 17% of the time I spent with my kiddos this week was in the shitter. I shit you not. Which is why when my kid is taking like nine million years to take a dump, I'm constantly asking, "Are you done yet, are you done yet, are you done yet, now are you done?" over and over and over again. Can you imagine someone sitting there asking you that repeatedly while you're trying to squeeze out a brown one? Helllllo, future constipation issues. It's just one more way I'm F'ing up my kids. Awesome.

One SINGLE trip to the bathroom with my kid

ME: Let's go try to use the potty.

HOLDEN: I don't have to.

ME: Let's just try. You haven't gone since you woke up.

HOLDEN: No, I don't have to.

ME: Well, *I'm* going now, so let's try.

HOLDEN: Only if you carry me.

ME: Fine.

(I just didn't feel like dealing, so I carried him in. Yeah, I know you're probably thinking he's going to grow up to be an entitled asshole because I carried him to the bathroom one time.)

HOLDEN: I want the big stall.

ME: It's taken. Here's one that's open.

HOLDEN: I want the big one.

ME: Fine.

(Again, I don't feel like arguing, so we wait a minute and it opens up.)

HOLDEN: What's this? What's this? What's this? What's this?

ME: Ewww, Holden, nooo, that's gross, that's where people throw their, uhhh, stuff. Don't touch that! Don't touch that!!!! I said DON'T TOUCH THATTTTT!

HOLDEN: I'm touching ittttt.

(Grrrrr.)

ME: Do you want to stand up or sit down?

HOLDEN:

ME: Do you want to stand up or sit down?

HOLDEN:

ME: Fine, I'll go first.

HOLDEN: *(as soon as I'm sitting on the potty)* NOOOOOO, I WANTED TO GO FIRST!!!!

ME: Then you should have gone.

HOLDEN: *(trying to push me off)* Wahhhhhhh, get off!!!

ME: Holden, stop it right now. I'm done. Stand up or sit down?

HOLDEN:

ME: Fine, here.

HOLDEN: NOOOOO, I WANTED TO SIT!!!

ME: Arrrghh, fine.

(As soon as he's sitting, Niagara Falls pours out of him.)

ME: I thought you didn't have to go.

HOLDEN: Do you hear that?

ME: Yes.

HOLDEN: I'm pooooping.

ME: Awesome.

(Like four minutes later, which doesn't really sound like that long, but go ahead and count out 240 seconds and then imagine doing that while you're standing in a public restroom with nothing to do but watch the bulging purple vein on your rugrat's forehead.)

ME: Are you done yet?

HOLDEN: No.

ME: Now are you done?

HOLDEN: No.

ME: NOW are you done?

HOLDEN: Do you smell that?

ME: Yes.

HOLDEN: Is it stinky?

ME: Yes.

HOLDEN: I'm done.

ME: Thank God. Bend over.

HOLDEN: No, I don't need to wipe.

ME: You do need to wipe. You pooped.

HOLDEN: No, I didn't poop.

ME: Yes, you did.

HOLDEN: NO, I DIDDDDDN'T!!!

ME: Look, there it is.

HOLDEN: There's two. One. Two.

ME: Yes, now bend over.

HOLDEN: That one looks like a crocodile.

ME: Totally. Now bend over.

(He puts his forehead on the bathroom floor. Awesome. Can you catch any diseases through your forehead? I unlock the door.)

HOLDEN: I WANTED TO UNLOCK IT!!

ME: Okay, unlock it.

(I relock it and wait while he tries to unlock it, but he can't figure it out.)

ME: Do you want my help?

HOLDEN: No.

(Insert the *Jeopardy* music here.)

ME: Can I help you, buddy?

HOLDEN: No.

ME: Here, lemme help.

(Thank God he lets me this time and doesn't pitch a fit.)

ME: Time to wash our hands.

HOLDEN: I don't have to.

ME: Yes, you do.

HOLDEN: No, I didn't touch anything.

ME: Yes, you did. And we always wash our hands after going potty.

HOLDEN: No.

ME: Yes.

HOLDEN: No.

ME: They will not let you leave this bathroom until you wash your hands. It's a rule.

(I don't know who the F "they" are, but he buys it.)

HOLDEN: Don't turn it on for me.

ME: You can't reach it. Do you want a lift?

HOLDEN: No.

(He tries to reach the sink handle for a while.)

ME: Can I help you?

HOLDEN: No. *(big pause)* Helpppp meeee!!!

ME: Now go ahead and wash them.

(He puts his hand under the soap dispenser.)

ME: You need water first.

(He ignores me.)

ME: Holden, the soap won't work without water.

(He still ignores me and starts to rub the soap without water, so I splash a little water into his hands.)

HOLDEN: Nooooo!!!!

ME: You need water. Rub it in. All over.

(He rubs the same spot on his palm for like 20 seconds.)

ME: The tops. Your fingers. All over. Twenty seconds.

HOLDEN: You count.

ME: 1, 2, 3, 4, 5, 6, 7, 8, 9, 10, 11, 12, 13, 14, 15, 16, 17, 18, 19, 20. Okay, rinse them off.

HOLDEN: Count to 100.

ME: No, that's good.

HOLDEN: Count to 100.

ME: 89, 90, 91, 92, 93, 94, 95, 96, 97, 98, 99, 100. *(He has no F'ing clue I started in the middle.)* Now wash them off.

(I have to lift him up like Superman so he doesn't touch the soaking-wet counter and get drenched.)

ME: Here's a paper towel.

HOLDEN: I wanted to get it.

(OMG, seeeeriously??? Can we pleeeease get out of here already?!!!)

ME: Fine, get it.

(He gets his own paper towel. AFTER I lift him up because he can't reach and AFTER I put him down because the

motion sensor won't work for him so I have to get it for him. Imagine that.)

ME: Now throw it in the trash.

HOLDEN: I want to keep it.

ME: It's dirty. Throw it in the trash.

(And he does and we finally walk out. And on the way out he drags his fingers along the wall of the public restroom. The wall that's probably been speckled with fecal matter at some time. Awesome.)

HUBBY: What took you so long?

I give him the look of death.

Oh yeah, and this happens multiple times a day.

Let the potty training begin!!

Introducing the newest Olympic event . . . Synchronized Pooping!!!

LA LA LA LA LAAAAAA, just walking to Zoey's bedroom to put some clothes away. I walk by my room. Normal. I walk by Holden's room. Normal. I walk by the bathroom. WTF? No, wait a sec, to seriously do this WTF justice, I need to increase the font size, bold the shit out of it, and add like a thousand exclamation marks.

WTF?!!!!!!!!!!!!!!!

Zoey and Holden are standing there wiping their tushies with toilet paper. Okay, now I know what you're thinking. You're thinking that the view of young kiddos wiping their *own* asses is better than a view of the Grand Canyon from a helicopter. And yup, that's usually right. But not this time. Remain calm, remain calm, remain calm, I tell myself. There has to be a reasonable answer.

ME: Hey guys. Whatcha doin'?

HIM: We're wiping.

HER: Because we pooped.

Okay, so far these answers are reasonably normal.

ME: You both pooped?

THEM: Yes.

ME: Like Zoey pooped and then waited until Holden was done so you could wipe at the same time?

HER: No.

HIM: We did it together!

HER: Yeah, we shared the potty.

Nooooooo. Seriously? Seeeeeriously??? I've been trying to teach you guys to share things for years and THIS is when you decide to start? But I have to know.

ME: *(fearful)* Whatta you mean you shared it?

HER: We shared it!

ME: How?

HER: We both got on.

I'm picturing him sitting on the potty with her behind him, you know, like the way they would ride a horse together or the log flume ride at an amusement park, only a totally different kind of log this time. Ewwwww. Are you kidding me? And *without* pants on. But then Zoey proceeds to show me how I'm wrong and how actually they both sat sideways on the potty with their backs to each other. Awwww, tush to tush. How cute. NOT.

HER: He pooped, and then I pooped, and then he pooped, and then I pooped.

Plop plop, fizz fizz, holy crap how F'ed up this is. I mean, I always wanted my rugrats to be close and do shit together. But AGGGHHHH, NOT LITERALLY!!!

ME: Guys, that's gross. Don't do that again.

THEM: Okay.

And they went off giggling together and we shall never speak of this again.

ZOEY: *My tummy hurts.*

ME: *Do you have to poop?*

ZOEY: *I don't want to go to school.*

ME: *Do you have to poop?*

ZOEY: *I'm not hungry.*

ME: *Do you have to poop?*

Seriously, one day I think this kid is going to grow up to think that going poop is the solution to EVERYTHING.

BOYFRIEND: *I'm just not sure this relationship is working out.*

ZOEY: *Maybe you have to poop.*

Sometimes the cat throws up on the carpet and I get really pissed off. But sometimes he throws up in the perfect place to teach my kids an important lesson about drinking too much and losing your dignity.

Well, that was fun. Not.

YAYYYYY, WE'RE GOING ON VACATION!!! Yippeeeee!!! And by yippee, what I really mean is would some scientific genius person pleeeease invent a teleporter machine already because getting on an airplane with kids sucks more ass than a porno about rim jobs. Oh shit, my grandma's reading this. Sorry, Grandma, I'm sure you don't know what a rim job is. It's when a man or woman eats another person's butt out. No, not like those people on that airplane that crashed into the mountains and had to literally eat each other's butt flesh to survive. I'm referring to when people lick each other's anuses (anae???). But I digress. Big time. What was I talking about again? Oh yeah, how much traveling with kids sucks.

Okay, so after clearing the TSA line with our kids, which is basically akin to winning an Olympic decathlon, my hubby and I high-five each other and head to the gate with the kiddos and hopefully all our bags, but who knows? Alls I know is that this time we weren't stopped for any weapons the kids stealthily packed when I wasn't looking and no one ran away while the hubby and I were putting our shoes back on. And after walking 2,000 miles to the last gate on earth, we finally get there.

ANNOUNCER: Boarding will begin for unimportant people who don't matter in a few minutes. If you are a member of our super-special elite exclusive club because you live out of a suitcase and our flight attendants know you by name, please feel free to glide across our red carpet that is really nothing more than an ugly red doormat we picked up at Home Depot.

A shitload of business people with TUMI bags and blank stares step across the glamorous red doormat and onto the jet bridge.

ANNOUNCER: In case you're wondering, people with small children are not allowed to board early anymore because really everyone hates your guts for ruining our flight and because airlines no longer do things that make sense.

ME: What group number are we?

HUBBY: Seventeen.

So we wait. And wait. And wait.

ANNOUNCER: Group seventeen may board now.

ZOEY: I have to go to the bathroom.

Really? That's interesting because I think I just asked you if you had to go to the bathroom like three minutes ago when we passed the ladies' room. And three minutes before that when we passed another ladies' room. And every ladies' room before that on our 2,000-mile walk here.

ME: You're gonna have to hold it, sweetie.

ZOEY: I can't!!

ME: You have to.

So we wait in the lonnnng line to get on the plane and finally get to our seats and Zoey's totally doing the pee-pee dance even though she claims she doesn't have to go anymore so my hubby drags her to the stinky lavatory and then he has to fight the flow of traffic to get back to our seats, at which point the kids put on their boxing gloves to see who gets the window seat even though we decided who gets it four days ago by flipping a coin until Zoey changed her mind and decided that she wants to sit in the window seat on the return flight because "last is best" and then Holden believed her that "last is best" so he wanted the window seat on the way home too so they started fighting and we never came to a conclusion and now neither of them can remember what we de-cided and wheeeee vacations are so fun!!! The good news is my hubby agrees to sit with the rugrats on the way there so I can sit in the single seat all alone drinking those adorable little bottles of awesomeness since I spent the last fourteen days packing our suitcases and remembering shit like the sound machine and four tubes of toothpaste since no one in our family uses the same kind. And this is when my hubby decides to ask me if I remembered Holden's blankie and I'm like yes, but are you F'ing kidding me? WTF could I do now if I didn't? And by the way this is a genius discussion to have in front of Holden because what if I had forgotten it and he heard this right before we are about to be stuck for three hours in a metal capsule with lots of surly business-people at 10,000 feet above the earth?

And finally the pilot says he's closing the door so we can pull back from the gate and right as he says this Holden decides to have a shit-fit because he wants to sit near Mommy.

ME: Awww, I'm sorry, buddy. Look, there aren't any open seats next to me.

PERSON IN MIDDLE SEAT NEXT TO ME: I'll switch with him if he wants.

ME: *(through gritted teeth)* I'll stab you with a pen if you offer that again.

But Holden's annoying whines are escalating and if you are on an airplane with little kids, you are legally required to do whatever the hell it takes to keep them happy, so we end up rearranging seats and Zoey refuses to move to the aisle seat so now the arrangement is Holden in the window seat, Zoey in the middle seat, me in the torture seat, and Greg in his own seat all alone already sleeping, and I'm seriously considering pushing the flight attendant button to see if we can find out if there's a divorce lawyer on board.

And finally we're up in the air and for the next two hours everyone is happy and quiet and not a pain in the ass at all and I take complete credit for this and think it is all due to my superb parenting skills and has nothing to do with the iPads that are loaded up with millions of *PAW Patrol*s and *Wild Kratts* and *Scooby-Doo*s and other shit that will rot their brains out but keep the friendly skies friendly.

Okay, so have you ever noticed that airplanes are always too hot or too cold? Seriously, they are never just right. And this plane feels like the super-freezing refrigerator section in Costco, the one you grab shit from and run out of as fast as humanly possible before you lose appendages. So I put some sweatshirts on the kids and tuck my arms into my shirt because of course I remembered to pack everyone's sweatshirt except for mine. Shit. Why can't I ever remember mine and forget someone else's? Not that it would really matter because then I would just give mine away.

Anyways, the rest of the flight is actually awesome and peaceful and I have a shitload of candy to shovel into the kids' faces between iPad episodes, because God forbid there's a split second of possible freak-out time. And then suddenly I can feel the plane starting to descend. Yayyy, we're almost there without any incidents.

Until . . .

HOLDEN: I don't feel good.

And I look over and sure enough he's sweating bullets because the plane is now 9,000 degrees but I didn't realize this because I wasn't wearing a sweatshirt and Holden's face looks kinda greenish and ruh-roh . . .

HOLDEN: My tummy hurts.

I grab a barf bag out of the seat pocket in front of me as fast as humanly possible and reach over Zoey just in time to catch the barf as it shoots out of his mouth at full force.

HOLDEN: *BARRRRFFFFFFFFFF!!!!!!!*

ZOEY: MOMMMMM, I CAN'T SEE THE IPAD!!! MOVVVVVVE YOUR ARM!!!!!! MOMMMMM, MOVVVVE, I CAN'T SEE!!!!!!!!!

Oh, I'm sorry, is my arm that's catching the projectile throw-up blocking you from seeing this *PAW Patrol* episode you've probably seen a thousand times? But she continues to scream and he continues to puke and I continue to reach my arm across her and my husband continues to sleep like a peaceful little jackass until the plane finally bumps down on the runway and my husband opens his eyes for the first time in three hours.

HUBBY: Wha—what happened? Are we here?

ME: Fuckface.

FYI, I didn't really say this out loud, but I can't tell you how much I wanted to.

I look over at Holden and he's turned back into a normal shade of peach and someone has finally turned his mouth faucet off.

ME: How ya doing, buddy?

HOLDEN: I feel a little better.

EVERYONE IN OUR SECTION OF THE PLANE: *(clapping and cheering for him)* Yayyyyyyy!!!

Apparently they'd all been listening to the throw-up fest in row 27 and when we stand up I expect people to pat me on the back and high-five me for doing such an awesome job, but for some reason they just keep smiling at Holden and saying, "Good job, buddy." Yes, by all means, good job at sitting there watching the iPad for three hours and projectile vomiting at 90 miles per hour. WTF?

ME: *Show me that cute tushy, Holden.*

HOLDEN: *Look at my cute penis.*

Ummm, no. For all sorts of reasons.

Shake it off, shake it off (and if that doesn't work, get a sponge)

PENIS, PECKER, PETER, SCHLONG, OR what I like to call it, the appendage I have no F'ing clue about. Don't get me wrong, I've seen my fair share of penises (hubby, if you're reading this, of course your gorgeous penis is the only one I've ever seen but I'm using literary license here). Anyways, what was I saying? Oh yeah, *I've seen penises.* But when I found out I was having a boy, one of my first thoughts was, nooooo, I don't know anything about the penis!!!

When Holden was a newborn, I quickly learned that when it comes to changing a diaper with a penis (OMG, my English teacher would KILL me for writing that because diapers do not have penises, but you know what I'm saying), there are really only three things you have to remember. (a) It doesn't matter whether you wipe front to back or back to front like it does on a girl. (b) Don't forget to lift the wrinkly elephant balls so you can clean under them. And (c) while you're doing all this, make sure you cover that junk up or you could be gargling a mouthful of pee-pee.

But then my little buddy got a little older and started using the potty and I started learning a whole lot more about how boys go to the bathroom. I mean my daughter was relatively simple. She climbed up there, went, wiped, and washed her hands just like me. My son, on the other hand . . . OMG, like a million things can go wrong when boys use the potty. So I present to you seven things that can go wrong when my son goes to the bathroom:

1. Okay, here's the dealio. Not to get too graphic, but if your kiddo is naked when he goes to the bathroom sitting down, everything is hunky dory because his legs straddle the potty and the penis automatically points down. Plinnnnk. Yes, that's the sound of a penis pointing down. Well, a small one. As they get older the sound is more like PLUNNNNK. But let's say he's wearing clothes and you don't want to spend ten minutes stripping your kiddo down before he slides up on that toilet seat. Well, then his pants are around his ankles and his legs are basically shackled together and his peeper is automatically in the up position and if you don't push that sucker down, you're looking at a rainbow of pee-pee straight onto your lap. And call me a prude, but I'm not really into golden showers. So whenever my son goes to the bathroom, I sound like a perverted broken record. "Push your penis down. Push your penis down. Push your penis down." And then if he doesn't push it down, I have to poke it down with my finger between his legs and ewwww, suddenly I feel like the pedophile who works in the back of the baseball card shop.

2. Alrighty then. Maybe you're like me and you didn't even know that little boys pee sitting down because pretty much my whole life alls I ever saw was men standing up and peeing and I was all fifty shades of green with envy. Wahhhh, why do I have to squat over the porta-potty until my thighs burn like they're on fire? I want a peeenis!! It's not fair! But little boys are different than men. Some little boys pee-pee sitting down. And some little boys pee-pee standing up. And some little boys, like my guy, like to decide which way to do it every stupid time and it's super annoying if you're their mom because basically their bladder is like a ticking time bomb that's going to explode and you have exactly three seconds to figure out whether they want to sit or stand before KABLOOOEY, there's a giant urine explosion. Fun times.

3. You know what's really fun? When my son is peeing standing up and my daughter says, "Hey Holden, look at this!!" and I don't know if his neck is broken or something but he decides to turn around with his whole body to look instead of just turning his head or looking with his eyes. Awesome. Yes, I do think this bathroom really does look nicer with a yellow drippy border.

4. And let's not forget about pooping.

   ME: Are you done, buddy? Bend over so I can wipe you.

   And then I have to throw the toilet paper in the potty off to the side so it doesn't cover the poop up and I say:

   ME: Want to see it before I flush?

Yes, this sounds all kinds of F'ed up, I know. But if he doesn't get to see it, here's what happens:

HOLDEN: WAHHHHHH!!!! I wanted to seeee it!!!!!

ME: You'll see it next time, kiddo.

HOLDEN: NOOOOOOOO, WHY DID YOU FLUSH IT??!!! YOU'RE THE WORST MOMMY EVERRRRR!!!! I WANT TO SEE IT NOWWWWW!!!!

ME: I can't bring it back.

HOLDEN: BRING IT BACCCCCK!!!!!

ME: Sorry, kiddo, there is no unflush on a toilet. Thank God.

I don't know WTF it is with men, but they like to check out their poop. Sometimes he's impressed that it's big, sometimes he likes to count the pieces, and sometimes he says it looks like some kind of animal. I guess I should just be glad he has a passion.

5.   Ohhh yeah, the Taylor Swift effect. Yo Tay Tay (I can call her that because we're best buds), I'll bet you didn't know that moms across America would be singing your tune to their boys after they take a leak. Well, maybe I'm the only one who does it, but every time my son's done peeing, I sing "shake it off, shake it off," because there's always one drop of pee-pee still clinging to the tip of my son's peeper and if he doesn't shake, it ends up dripping onto the floor or onto the seat or onto me, and I know it's just one tiny drop of urine but it's the principle, ya know?

6. Oh, here's another phenomenon (holy crap was that a hard word to type) that only happens to boys. After a giant fight over whether to sit or stand, he's finally sitting up on the potty, everything is looking good, and suddenly I'm like, are you kidding me? Why is there a little river of pee-pee going down the outside of the potty? Awww shit, my kid has such good aim, he manages to shoot it right out that one little crack between the toilet bowl and the toilet seat. Grrrr.

7. Okay, I don't know WTF my toddler is thinking about (Minnie Mouse naked and doing the hot dog dance???), but did you know that two-year-olds get woodies? And I'm not talking about the cool cowboy dude from *Toy Story*. Hellllllo, earth to God, do babies seriously need to get boners? Because I'll tell you what sucks. When my son has to go pee-pee and he can't because his wee-willy-winky is pointed at the ceiling and we have to wait for it to go down. Come on, kiddo, think of something gross. Think about Caillou's mom naked.

Anyways, that's probably a good note to end on. If you are reading this before bed, I highly recommend looking at something else before you go to sleep so you don't have nightmares about Mama Caillou's naked floppy boobs and vajayjay. I mean no, I've never seen her vajayjay, but if I had to guess, it's as doughy as the rest of her and ewwwwww.

The difference between girls and boys:

(Looking in toilet)

HER: *Ewwww!*

HIM: *Corn!!*

HOLDEN: *I pee-pee out of my penis.*

ME: *Yes.*

HOLDEN: *You pee-pee out of your penis.*

ME: *I don't have a penis. I have a vagina.*

HOLDEN: *Daddy has a 'gina.*

ME: *No, Daddy has a penis.*

HOLDEN: *Zoey pee-pees out of her penis.*

ME: *Zoey doesn't have a penis. She has a vagina.*

HOLDEN: *You have a penis and a 'gina.*

ME: *No, I just have a vagina.*

HOLDEN: *Zoey has a penis and a 'gina.*

ME: *No, just a vagina.*

HOLDEN: *I have a penis and Daddy has a penis.*

ME: *Yup.*

HOLDEN: *And you have a 'gina and Zoey has a 'gina.*

ME: *That's it, buddy. You've got it!*

HOLDEN: *Can I see your penis?*

WTF?

I Tried the Crying It Out Method...
I'M STILL CRYING

OKAY, YOU KNOW WHAT I HATE? WHEN LITTLE Miss Braggypants decides to tell me how her badass kids slept through the night at like two months old and how she doesn't understand why all these parents bitch and moan about not getting enough sleep. I'm like, helllllllo brainiac, there's a reason Starbucks is popping up on every block all over the world. It's not because people like to spend half their paychecks on fancy coffee drinks. It's because most parents are so F'ing tired every morning they literally can't function enough to make a 16-cent cup of coffee in their house. And I know you think you're all high and mighty because your brilliant techniques made your baby sleep through the night, but I am 200% convinced that you just got a good sleeper. Because guess what? I sleep trained too. And one of my kids sleeps like a narcoleptic who downed a bottle of Ambien, and the other one wakes me up like every ten minutes.

Bedtime is for succcccckers

SO I KNOW I'M SUPPOSED TO BE writing my own book and shit, but my three-year-old son, Holden, offered to write a chapter and I'd be an idiot not to say yes. I mean writing this thing has been a bitch, and I don't get paid unless it's a certain number of words, which means I might have to start writing really long sentences and saying things that don't matter like talking about random stuff like the trees and superheroes and toys and unicorns and making it weave into the story somehow so you can't tell that I'm just attempting to reach a certain number of words by going on and on and on and on a lot longer than I should about subjects so that I hit the number of words this is supposed to be and they pay me. Shit, that sentence was so long and pointless I can't remember WTF I was saying. Oh yeah, Holden offered to write a chapter and I said yes. I mean I basically give all my money to my kids anyways, so let's let him earn it. And I know you're only three, kiddo, but it better be a long chapter, like at least one thousand words. So anyways, here goes. A little chapter written by Holden Alpert:

Okay, even though we're toddlers and think stupid shit like eleventeen is a real number and rainbow is an actual color and

Caillou isn't a whiny douchebag, we're pretty much geniuses (geniae???) when it comes to stalling tactics at bedtime. I'm talking about some seriously brilliant shit. So I've polled a bunch of my toddler buddies and come up with a list of awesome ways to avoid going to bed at night. If you're a toddler and your mommy was stupid enough to leave this book within your reach, get ready to take some notes. Here is a bunch of kickass ways to stall at bedtime:

1. Let's start with a good one. After your mommy tucks you in and leaves, drop something on the floor, like a book or a toy or something. Something that'll make a large *THUD*. Then come out of your room complaining that you bumped your head and you need a kiss. Your mommy'll be all panicky and won't want you to go back to sleep until she's watched you a while to make sure you're behaving okay. Just don't push it and act too tipsy because the last thing you want is a trip to the ER.

2. Step one: Say you're thirsty. Step two: Watch your mommy cave because she can't deny you water without feeling like a total child abuser. Step three: Tip back that dinky cup of water and drink. And drink. And drink. And drink. Until she finally realizes you've been drinking nothing but air for the past thirty seconds. Muhahahahaha, you have now gotten to stay up thirty seconds longer. Suckkkkker.

3. So have you ever noticed that human beings do not come in the color clear? And you know what's awesome about that? Your mom can't see inside your body. And that's awesome be-

cause your mom will have no idea whether there's poop in you or not. So just back that tush up onto the toilet and cop a squat for as long as you want. And then grunt a little and say stuff like, "It feels like there's still poop inside me." And there's nothing she can do but wait.

4. Okay, I just got out my stopwatch and timed myself, so listen up, buttmunches. Do you know that it is physically impossible to do "Five Little Monkeys" in less than 28 seconds? But "Row, Row, Row Your Boat" can be sung in 3.5 seconds. I shit you not. Whatever you do, do NOT whine and beg for "one more song." Whine and beg for one more *specific* song.

5. When you call Mommy back into your room and she sounds totally pissed off because she hasn't had a moment to herself all day, just say this.

TODDLER: Mommy?

MOMMY: (*through gritted teeth*) What?!

TODDLER: Can I have one more kiss?

Watch her soften up like a stale Chips Ahoy in the microwave. She's not allowed to get mad or say no. It's the law.

6. To those of you brainiacs who aren't potty trained yet but should be, nice work 'cause you've got a weapon in your ARSE-nal. Yup, it's poop, and here's what you've gotta do. Hold that shit in (it's a skill that only the most professional toddlers have mastered) until right when your mommy is shutting your bedroom door. And as soon as she starts to leave, let

out a grunt or two to let her know you're serious. Bada-bing bada-BM, you've bought yourself at least five more minutes while she cleans that shit up and puts on a new pull-up.

7. Speaking of tushies, flaunt it if you've got it. You know how if you swing a pocket watch in front of someone's eyes, it can hypnotize them? Mommies are basically the same way if you wiggle a naked tushy in front of them. So drop those diapers and wiggle, wiggle, wiggle. Before she knows it, it'll be midnight and she'll be like, "Aggghhh, it's so late! Damn that cute tushy!!"

8. Okay, maybe you don't know it yet, but there's a serious art form to picking the right book at bedtime.

   TODDLER: Heyyy, I'm gonna pick this book because it's the longest one.

   Ennnnh, rookie mistake. Because before you know it, Mommy has skipped like nine pages and a million words and she's saying, "The End," and you're like, WTF, I thought I picked a long book. The key is to pick a long book that you have MEMORIZED. That way if she skips a word, you can be like, "Heyyyy, where the F is the part where the fish falls into the teapot?!!" And make sure to wait at least five pages before you tell her she missed it so she has to go back.

9. **MOMMY:** Good night.

   TODDLER: I forgot to say my prayers.

   She can't say no. If she does, she's basically saying if anything happens to you or your loved ones tonight, it's her fault and she's okay with going to hell.

10. Alright, this one takes a little planning in advance, so it's only for the most advanced toddlers, but here's what you've gotta do. Is there something special you sleep with? Like a lovey or a blankie or that sharp sword that your mom let you sleep with once for a special treat but then you insisted on sleeping with it for the next two years. Hide that shit. Like shove it way under the couch or leave it in the trunk of the car or at the bottom of the hamper. Then when it's time for bed, ask for it. "Wahh-hhh, I can't sleep without my Pookie Bear!!!!!" Then sit back, watch, and enjoy the show of Mommy and Daddy turning the entire house upside down searching desperately for it. And whatever you do, accept NO substitutes.

11. Yes, I know ten is a nice number to end on, but who the hell decided ten should be the magic number? So here's #11. If it gets really bad, pull out the big guns. Say you're worried that if you go to sleep, you're going to die. That or cry so hard you throw up all over yourself.

ME: *Holden, you did a great job sleeping last night!!*

HOLDEN: *Uhhh-ohhhh.*

ME: *What is it?*

HOLDEN: *I forgot to wake you up.*

How NOT to keep your kiddo awake in the car

ME: Let's go, let's go, let's go! Everyone to the car right now!

HOLDEN: But I'm in the middle of my ice cream.

ZOEY: And I have to go poop.

ME: Holden, take your last lick. Zoey, suck that turtlehead back in.

People in the restaurant are looking at me like I'm a total nutjob, but we are already super late and if we're not in the car in five minutes, Holden is going to fall asleep on the car ride home and then he won't take a *real* nap later and then I'm not going to be able to shower and it is highly probable that if I lift one of my arms the BO is literally going to kill all the people within a tenfoot radius and then I'm going to be thrown in jail for murder. So no, I am not overreacting. We have to leave RIGHT F'ING NOW.

ME: No lollygagging, guys, let's go!!

Awww crap, did I just use the word *lollygagging*? Excuse me while I kick my own ass for being such a dorkwad.

So I throw the kids in the car as fast as humanly possible and buckle Holden's seat belt, but I do it too quickly and I accidentally pinch his peeper and now he's screaming his head off and I have to slow down and turn into the nicest mommy in the whole world and apologize a thousand times to help him forget about the fact that I just scarred him for life.

ME: I'm sooooo sorry, buddy!!! I didn't mean to!!!!

HOLDEN: Wahhhhh, kiss it!!!!!!!!!

ME: No, sweetie, I can't kiss it.

HOLDEN: WAHHHHHHHHH, KISSSSSS ITTTTTTT!!!!

ME: Mommy cannot kiss your penis, honey.

Things I never thought I'd have to say. But after he screams for like a thousand more minutes I finally come up with a solution and I kiss my hand and I pat his peeper and I guess that's good enough because he stops screaming finally and I get into the car and start to drive home. But when I glance in the rearview mirror that I have angled slightly down at that perfect angle that lets me see the road AND the kiddos, Holden's eyes look totally heavy. Awwww shit, nooooo, don't sleep yet!! I start asking him questions at a mile a minute to keep him awake.

ME: Holden, do you see that truck?! Holden, look out your window. Look at that car carrier! Holden, keep your eyes open! Oooooh, Holden, look at that blue car! It's like a race-

car. Look, it's a puppy. Holden! Holllldennnnn. Wake up!
Wake up! Wake up! Don't fall asleep yet, buddy. Look, it's a
cement mixer!!!

And I'm driving super fast, but I'm hitting every red light, and
I'm blaring the music and I'm even pumping the brake super
hard at red lights to make the car jump like one of those lowrider
cars that bounces because I'm hoping that will keep him awake,
but it's totally not working and his eyes are about to close.

ZOEY: (*sounding a lot like a poltergeist*) RAWRRRRRRRRR,
HOLDEN WAKE UPPP!!!!!!!!!!!!!!!!!

ME: Don't do that, sweetie.

But I see his eyes open for a split second, so I change my mind.

ME: Wait, yes, do that!! Do that!!!

So Zoey keeps screaming at him and I have no idea how anyone can sleep through all this but apparently he can even though
this is the same kid who wakes up in the middle of the night if the
neighbor coughs next door. WTF? His eyelids flutter closed and
3, 2, 1 . . . he's out. Shit. Now the best thing I can hope for is to
drive around quietly and let him sleep for a while before we go
home so he's not a sleep-deprived maniac later today. So I turn
toward the highway and give Zoey the *shhhh* finger in the mirror.
And we're driving quietly, until suddenly out of nowhere . . .

ZOEY: Look, Mom!! A coyote!

At first I'm like ennnnhhh, bullshit, but I look up and sure enough, standing in the middle of the circular ramp to the highway there's a coyote on the grass.

ME: Wow, that's weird, it *is* a coyote! Cool.

HOLDEN: What? What is it?!!

Awww shit, look who just woke up after a very restful three-minute nap.

ZOEY: It's a coyote, Holden!

No, no, noooo, don't say it!!! Because I don't know how highways are where you live, but where we live, you drive very fast on them, and we're already flying at fifty miles per hour on the highway and that coyote is lonnnnng gone. Shit.

HOLDEN: Where is it? I wanna see it!!

ZOEY: You missed it!

ME: Ohhh, I'm sorry buddy, we already passed it.

Shit shit shit. This is not going to go well at all.

ZOEY: It was sooooo cool, Holden!!! It was GIANT! And it was growling.

Ummm, no it wasn't. It was standing there doing nothing.

ZOEY: He was like this, "Grrrrrrrrrr," and he was as big as a lion!

WTF?

HOLDEN: Go back!!! I wanna see the coyote!!!

Yeah, okay, I'll just get off at the next exit in two miles and turn around and travel three miles back and then get off to turn around again and then go back to the entrance ramp and he'll probably still be standing there in the same spot. Not.

ME: I'm sorry, Holden, we can't.

HOLDEN: GOOOO BACKKKK!!!!

ME: We can't, buddy. But let's keep our eyes out for another one!!

Because you know, the highways are just lined with random coyotes.

HOLDEN: NOOOOO, GOOOOO BACK!!!!!! I *(air suck)* WANT *(air suck)* TO *(air suck)* SEE *(air suck)* THE *(air suck)* COYO-TEEEEE *(air suck)*!!! WAHHHHHHHHHHHHHHHHHHHHHH-HHHHHHHHHHHHHHHHHHHHHHHHHHHHHHHHHHHHH-HHHHHHHHHHHH!!!!!!! *(huge-ass air suck)*

And in case it isn't clear based on the number of H's in the word *wah*, this goes on for the rest of the ride until we're four blocks from home, at which point he suddenly stops screaming and the car goes silent and he falls asleep. Phew, finally. And at least he'll get a two-minute nap in now. No wait, F that, I'll just park the car and stay with him while he naps and surf on my phone and Zoey can go inside and watch TV. Brilliant! I pull up the driveway and open the garage door. The garage door that really never seemed very loud until this moment.

GARAGE DOOR: EERRRRGGHHHHHHHHHHHHHHHHH-HHH!!!!!!!!!!!

HOLDEN: WAHHHHHHHHHHHHHHHHHHHHHHHHHHH-HHHHHHHHHHHHHHHHHHHHHHHHHHHHHHHHHHH-HHHHH, I WANT TO SEE THE COYOTE!!!!!!!!!!!!!!!!!!!!

Awesome.

I loⱱⱱⱱⱱⱱⱱe sleepoⱱers . . . when they're at somebody else's house

Dear friend who's taking my kiddo for a sleepover tonight,

Here are some rules for it. Yeah, that's right, rules for YOUR house. Because she's coming back home to MY house tomorrow, and I don't need you F'ing up all the hard work I've put into her over the past six years. So here goes.

1. *If she wakes up in the middle of the night, you have my permission to tell her to "go the F back to sleep." Just make sure the last words you say as you shut the door are something nice like, "night night, honey" or "sweet dreams." You know, just in case it's the last thing she hears. That's what I do.*

2. *Please do not cuddle with her or rub her back while she falls asleep. (a) That's creepy, and (b) she's gonna come back to my house asking for that shit and, well, homey don't play that.*

3. *Please don't show her any scary movies or TV shows. Because if she comes home having nightmares about Chucky or Freddy or the Zombiepocalypse, I'll tell you what I'm gonna do. The next time your kid comes to our house for a sleepover, I'm going*

to get her nice and addicted to
Caillou before I send her back.

4. *If your kid doesn't sleep in*
underwear, that's cool. For
your kid. My kid sleeps in
underwear. Period. There are
three orifices down there and
they need to be contained.

5. *If she says something like, "My mommy doesn't make me*
brush my teeth" or "At home I'm allowed to," I fully expect you
to send her home where she can do these things. And by "do
these things," what I really mean is get her ass kicked by me for
lying and making me look like a shitty mom.

6. *Please do not let her drink a gallon of water before bed. She will*
try. She will complain that she's thirsty. She will be relentless.
She will not, however, pay you back for the mattress she ruins
if you can't tell her no.

7. *Don't cook her like the biggest, best-*
est breakfast in the whole wide
world, like chocolate chip pancakes
with extra chocolate chips buried
under a mountain of whipped
cream. The goal is to make her like
you, not to make her like you MORE
than she likes me.

8. *Please do not let her sleep with the lights on. Unless you are in fact offering to pay our electric bill for the next two years, in which case, do whatever the hell you want.*

9. *Yeah, I know that she might stay up a little late giggling and shit, but please don't let her stay up till all hours of the night. 'Cause if she comes home acting like a monster tomorrow, I'm coming back to your house because I forgot something—to leave my over-exhausted kid there.*

10. *If I forgot to pack her an extra pair of underwear and you lend her a pair, don't expect them back for a while. Even if I see you a bunch of times. Because if we're in front of other people, I'm not handing you a pair of little girl's panties. That's how rumors get started.*

11. *If you need me to pick her up for any reason, don't hesitate to call me. AFTER 8:00 a.m. tomorrow.*

That's it. Hope it's a blast!!

> *Love,*
> *The mom whose ringer will be off tonight*

Sometimes he transitions to his bed no problem. And sometimes I desperately need my afternoon "me" time and hell if I'm taking the risk.

HOLDEN: *I don't want these sheets!*

ME: *I'll change them tomorrow buddy.*

HOLDEN: *I HATE them!*

ME: *I promise we'll change them first thing tomorrow.*

HOLDEN: *I'm going to pee on them tonight.*

ME: *Well then you'll be cold and wet until TOMORROW WHEN I CHANGE THEM!!!*

Let the 3 a.m. standoff begin. You're F'ing with the wrong mommy, kiddo.

Reasons my kid wakes me up and what I say back, sometimes out loud and sometimes in my head

"I need water." (Why, so you can pee in your bed?)

"My legs hurt." (I hurt everywhere. Quit being a pussy.)

"The closet door is open a crack." (Because the monster is watching you to make sure you go to sleep.)

"I want my door open." (So you can hear *The Walking Dead* or me and Daddy doin' the nasty? Umm, no.)

"I need more stuffed animals in my bed." (You sleep in a claw machine.)

"I didn't want this in my bed." (Step 1: Throw it out. Step 2: Get brain checked for stupidity.)

"Look at this booger." (Look at this middle finger.)

"My finger smells." (Stop scratching your butt.)

"I forgot to brush my teeth." (The sooner the tooth fairy will come.)

"The cat is in here." (Lucky you, a real live stuffed animal!)

"I need to pee." (Welcome to my world.)

"I need to poop." (How is that possible? You didn't even eat today.)

"My covers fell off." (Then you'll be cold until you put them back on, won't you?)

"My belly hurts." (Do you have to toot?)

"My belly still hurts." (Do you have to poop?)

"I tooted." (I'll call the press.)

"I want my socks off." (How on earth will we ever solve this problem?)

"I want my socks on." (Sure, I can help you do that. Tomorrow morning.)

"I want my socks on my hands." (Things nutjobs say for 400, Alex.)

"I had a nightmare." (Amazing, since you weren't even sleeping yet.)

"What's that shadow?" (It's a shadow.)

"I heard a sound." (Did it sound like a toddler being a whiny bitch? 'Cause that's what I hear.)

"I want to sleep with you." (You sound like your father.)

"I want you to sleep with me." (You're gonna say that to a lot of girls throughout the years and they're going to say no. Consider this practice.)

"I want my Thomas pajamas." (I want my old boobs back.)

"Hi." (Good-bye.)

"I love you." (If you did, you wouldn't be doing this.)

"I'm tired." (FU.)

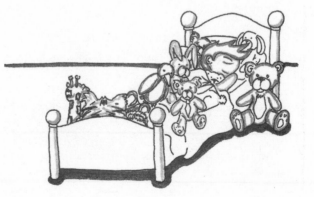

Seriously, kid? You need like three books, nine songs, four sips of water, and to be tucked in perfectly with your stuffed animals all around you before you'll go to bed at night, but you can fall asleep sitting up at the table? WTF? I give up.

ME: Okay, kiddo, here are your choices. You can totally drop your nap now and never give me a break all day until I literally go insane and kill myself and then you won't have a mommy for the rest of your life, OR you can keep napping until you're in kindergarten and then you get to keep having a mommy. It's up to you. Mommy or no Mommy?

How the F to Entertain
Your Rugrats When You Have
NOTHING TO DO

DO YOU KNOW WHO INVENTED TELEVISION? NO, neither do I. Which is probably a good thing, because if I knew I would tackle him and hug him to death when I run into him in heaven one day. Just kidding, I know they're not letting me in those Pearly Gates and really Satan has a blender full of margaritas waiting for me. But I digress. Anyways, back to our discussion about the most important thing on earth: television. Here's the thing. Even though I'm constantly wondering how much screen time is a good amount for my kiddos, zero hours has never been an option. Like when I'm flying with them on an airplane, I'm like holy shit, I can't believe parents used to do this without iPads. Or when I'm playing a riveting game of Barbies with my daughter and I'm surfing on my phone at the same time, sometimes I stop and wonder whether parents literally died of boredom before there were smartphones. Screen time helps me be a better mom and not kill myself. So thank you for saving my life, screen time. Me love you long time.

Dear *Sesame Street*,
I LOVVVVVVE you

Dear Sesame Street,

Hi! How are you? So I've been meaning to write you for a long time, but my to-do list is always like nine miles long, and I'm finally just getting a chance to sit down and do it. I just wanted to say thank you. Hmm, that doesn't quite do it justice. What I mean is THANK YOUUUU!!!!!!!! You are single-handedly responsible for sooooo much awesome shit in my life. (Shit, did I just curse to Sesame Street? That can't be right.)

Anyways, here goes. Thank you so much for letting me shower like a million times. Well, not a million, but at least once every three days for the past five years. I can't tell you how many times I've plopped my kids in front of a good episode of Sesame Street *so that I can stand under the hot water knowing they probably won't barge in to ask me for something annoying or to point at my tush and laugh or to build a log cabin out of my tampons (wrapped UNused ones, in case you have the wrong image in your head). I thank you and so do all the people who sit within a ten-foot radius of me at Starbucks.*

Also thank you so much for teaching my kids their numbers. Before I had kiddos, I always thought I'd be one of those moms who'd sit at the kitchen table (actually, I always pictured a giant granite island in a big fancy mansion, but that didn't happen) with my rugrats and we'd do math and reading and flash cards together, but alas, I am not that mom. I mean once I bought this big kindergarten workbook at Costco, but the spine has yet to be cracked. But thanks to the Count and Feist's counting song on Sesame Street, *my kids weren't total idiots when they started school.*

Oh, and while we're on the subject of THS (Television Home-schooling), thank you for teaching my kiddos some awesome vocab words. Words like camouflage, absorb, *and* identical. *If it weren't for* Word on the Street, *all my kids would know are bad four-letter words that aren't gonna do jack shit for them on the SATs. Although come to think of it, I actually did say the F word quite a bit when I was taking the SATs.*

Oh yeah, here's another thing I need to thank you for. Thank you SOOOO much for keeping me somewhat up to date on Holly-wood. Because here's the thing. When you've got little kiddos, you don't see movies anymore, so you have no F'ing clue who the big celebs are. I mean, I open up People *magazine these days and I'm like, "Don't know her," "Who the hell is that?" and "I can't believe they don't have a single picture of Shannen Doherty in this issue." And then I turn on* Sesame Street *for my rugrats and I'm like, "Ohhhhh, that's who Anna Kendrick is." Someone was talking about her the other day and I was like,* who? *The next time I'll actually be able to say something and not stand there looking like a mute codfish.*

Oh, and Ses? Can I call you that? Thank you so much for NOT being a cartoon. There are wayyyy too many cartoons these days and I know it's just my opinion but cartoons pretty much suck ass. Like here are some of the cartoons that are out there: Caillou, *the Whiniest Douchenugget on earth;* Bubble Guppies, *whose name alone grates on my every nerve; and* Dora the Explorer, *who sounds like a broken record and who speaks with giant . . . . annoying . . . . pauses. I mean yeah, that little Abby Crap-dabby stuff is in there, but she'll always play second fiddle to Elmo. La la la, this is my song, I love Elmooo.*

Anyways, that's it. You F'ing rock, Sesame Street. I'd kiss you but kissing a TV set is kinda weird and yeah, I'm a little wacky but I'm not a total wackjob.

xoxoxoxoxoxoxoxoxoxoxoxoxoxoxoxoxoxoxoxoxoxo,
A mom who couldn't do it without you

HOLDEN: *I want more milk.*

ME: *What's the magic word?*

HOLDEN: *Meeska mooska Mickey Mouse.*

It's up to you:
die of boredom or die of Ebola

THIS IS ME IN AUGUST:

Okay, so Holden has soccer on Mondays, school on Tuesdays and Thursdays, gymnastics on Fridays, and I think I'm just gonna leave Wednesdays open so we have some free time to do some nice stuff together. I mean it's not like he's gonna be little forever and I want to have some special mommy-son time.

AND THIS IS ME IN OCTOBER:

AGGGHHHHHH, what was I thinking?!!! He's up and it's only 6:15 a.m. and WTF are we going to do for FIVE hours until lunchtime?!!! Quick, someone give me a time machine so I can go back to August and kick my ass for being such a moron and thinking unscheduled time would be a nice thing. Because here are our choices for places we can spend our "special" time on Wednesdays and why all of them pretty much suck donkey balls.

Any Place with a Ball Pit

So once I saw this cool time-lapse video on how they clean a ball pit and they literally emptied out the pit and then picked up each ball and sprayed it with some organic cleaner fluid and wiped it down carefully and slowly refilled the pit one ball at a time. I guess it was supposed to make you feel like ball pits are totally clean as a whistle, but here's what I took from it. Cleaning the ball pit is a HUGE pain in the ass so they pretty much only do it like once a year. And you just know like two minutes after they clean it, little Petey with the incontinence problem is gonna jump in there and take care of the cleanliness in one fell swoop. Or rather in one fell poop.

PETEY: Mommy, I went potty in the balls. (*Hmm, that sounds kinda wrong.*)

MOMMY: Quick, let's get the hell out of here before anyone finds out.

And then my kid jumps in right after. "Mommy, my socks are wet!" Ewwwww.

One of Those Tree House Climby Places

Do you guys have one of these places where you live? It's like this big giant tree house play area where the kids can run around and play while the parents basically sit on benches and watch them. In theory, it is AWESOME. But here's what really happens.

SOME DOUCHEBAGGY NANNY: Ooooh, this is great because I can totally just yap on my cell phone for eight hours a day while that rugrat I'm supposed to watch runs around. I can't believe I'm getting paid to do this!!!

Yo Nanny McFartface, your crapmuffin just pushed my kid out of the way so he could climb *UP* the slide and karate chop some poor little toddler and now he's shoving his hand so far up his nose, he's giving himself brain surgery and then wiping his boogers on that sleeping baby over there. Get off your F'ing phone!!!! Of course, I don't really say this to her because I'm not brave enough, so I just spend my time throwing eye daggers at her that she doesn't ever notice.

Going for a Walk

Wahooooo, the weather is nice enough to take a walk. Let's go to the park, kiddo!

KIDDO: Look at that dog. Look at that flower. Look at that fire hydrant. Look at that weed. Look at that crack. Look at that trash. I'm gonna pick up that trash.

ME: Nooo, don't pick up the trash!

KIDDO: Now I'm gonna lick my gross hand. Look at that sign. Look at that blade of grass. Look at that lawn mower. Look at that dog. Are we at the park yet?

ME: Umm no, we are LITERALLY standing on the first cement square of our path and haven't taken a step yet.

The Children's Museum

I kinda think the entire purpose of the Children's Museum is to see how many grimy little children can put their grubby little paws on exactly the same button or xylophone or fake banana before

someone cleans it. Like seriously. What color is a banana? Yellow. What color is a banana at the Children's Museum? Gray. So I have this little rule in my house. If we are going on a vacation in the next two weeks, we are not allowed to go to the Children's Museum. Because within fourteen days of visiting the Children's Museum, someone in our house has giant amounts of green snot pouring out of their nose or giant amounts of green throw-up pouring out of their mouth.

Let's Just Stay at Home and Have Some Good Quality Playtime Together

Ennnnh, wrongo. Because you're playing *dollies* or *trucks* or *Spiderman fights Darth Vader* or *mermaid princess unicorns* or some other boring-as-shit game and you look at your watch to see if it's lunchtime yet and you're like, holy crap, how is it possible that we've only been playing for four minutes?!! I swear my playroom is some weird kind of time warp zone where time ticks . . . by . . . more . . . slowly . . . than . . . anywhere . . . else . . . in . . . the . . . world.

Shopping at Target

Well, thank God there's at least one place that knows my kid wakes up at the ass-crack of dawn so they open early. I LOVE YOU TARJAYYYY!!! But as much as I love Tarjay, here's some of the shit that happens there.

ME: No, you cannot sit in the big part of the cart, you have to sit in the seat. No, you cannot stand on the back of the cart. Fine, whatever, ride under the cart. At least you're not taking up precious cart space.

And then ten minutes later, he's all, "I wanna ride in the seat!!" And I'm like WTF, I just put all my shit in there. Fiiiine, I'll move it. And he sits down in the seat but after about ten minutes he's freaking out because he wants to leave but I still haven't picked up the one tiny thing I came for. "Just one more thing, buddy." And before I know it, I've picked up twelve more things and he's freaking out and drooling and screaming and we've only made it halfway through the store and we have to go check out before he spontaneously combusts.

CASHIER: Hello!! How are you today? Would you like to get a REDcard? It can save you 5%! And it benefits your child's school! Did you find everything you need? How was your shopping experience? Oooh, have you tried this soup before? Is it tasty? Do you need any gift receipts today? What's your son's name? He's a cutie.

Yes, Mr. Chippy, this is definitely a good time to chat since I'm just a wee bit occupied trying to peel my kid off the floor and pry open his clenched fingers that are wrapped around a lip balm he's trying to steal from the impulse area. I appreciate that you are just trying to be nice, but just put the F'ing stuff in the F'ing bag so we can get the F out of here before someone dies.

And just for shits and giggles, here are a few more of my favorites

VISITING A FARM

Yes, let's go pet animals that roll around in their own poop and then put our fingers in our mouths while our moms yell at us to "WAIT!!! I HAVE HAND SANITIZER!!!"

THE LIBRARY

Let's go to a place where kids are supposed to be quiet (bwha-hahahahaha). And how is it possible that every time I check the library calendar to see when story hour is, it was yesterday? I swear someone is spying on me and every time I think about going there, they change the day just to F with me.

BOUNCE HOUSE OR TRAMPOLINE PLACE

This is actually an AWESOME place to take your kids. As long as you have a lot of time to hang out at the ER afterward.

Annnnd the moral of this story is that annoying moms who over-schedule the crap out of their kids are actually F'ing brilliant and the only reason I make fun of them is because I'm jealous.

Yo Pinterest, check this shit out. Some kids play with iPads when they go to a restaurant, and some kids make Elsa's cape out of panty liners. Bam!

ME: *And on that farm he had a . . .*

ZOEY: *Squid.*

ME: *Pick an animal that makes a sound, Zoey. And on that farm he had a . . .*

ZOEY: *Octopus.*

ME: *One that makes a noise.*

ZOEY: *Turtle.*

ME: *Nope.*

ZOEY: *Deer.*

ME: *Can't you think of one farm animal that makes a noise?*

ZOEY: *A bunny.*

ME: *That doesn't make a noise.*

ZOEY: *Yes it does. Hop hop.*

This kid is either lacking in the brain department or she's so crazy smart, she knows exactly what to say to annoy the shit out of me.

Peeew peeew peeewww and other sounds that make me want to chop my ears off

DO YOU EVER GO SOMEWHERE, like to a recital or on an airplane, and think, holy crap, how the hell did parents handle times like this before portable electronic devices? Like when I think about those dudes crossing the country in covered wagons moving west with their rugrats, I'm like, how the hell did you not kill yourself? The game I Spy wasn't even invented yet. And even if it was, how many times can you spy a tree or a mountain or a dirt road? Are we there yet? Are we there yet? Are we there yet? Are we there yet? Times like ten million. I mean being scalped by Native Americans sucks ass, but you haven't been tortured until you try to get over the Rocky Mountains in a covered wagon full of toddlers.

So am I in favor of letting kids use electronic devices? Hells yeah.

I mean sure, I'm all for talking to each other and reading real books and shit, but when you have a four-hour plane ride with two douchenuggets who didn't come with volume buttons and you're surrounded by overworked flight attendants and hostile businessmen, this is not the time to bond with your rugrats. You're lucky if you don't tear each other apart limb by limb. You are not in *Little House on the Prairie*, and electronic devices are going to get you through this alive.

Like once I went on this long plane ride and this total Sanctimommy was sitting in front of us on the plane and she was all . . .

SANCTIMOMMY: No, kids, you know you only get screen time on Saturdays. I didn't even bring the iPad with me so you wouldn't be tempted.

Cut to thirty minutes later when both kids are playing a game of *Who can screech the loudest?* and Sanctimommy has thrown herself across the people in the exit row and is desperately trying to open the emergency hatch so she can throw herself out of the plane and the people in that row aren't even fighting her because they're debating whether it might in fact be the best option right now.

Now this would be a good time to break out the iPad. Could I have loaned her one of mine? Sure. But it's Wednesday!! And remember, no screen time on Wednesdays. Plus, watching Sanctimommy's shit-show was more entertaining than the shitty sitcom they were showing on the drop-down TVs. Hmmm, I wonder what ever happened to her. I'm guessing she's living out the rest of her days in a padded cell somewhere, replaying Pinterest projects in her head.

So is it okay to let your kiddo get in some good lack-of-quality screen time when you're out and about in a public space? F yeah.

But here's the thing: don't be a douchebag about it.

YOU: What?!!! But I thought letting my kid play Space Invaders while we were at Starbucks was the nice thing to do so he wouldn't bother everyone around us.

Uhhhh, mayyybe. Is he playing it with headphones? Is he playing it on like the lowest volume possible? Because if every person in a twenty-foot radius has to listen to *peeew peeew peeeew* for like thirty minutes straight, you're being a shartrag.

Because you, my dear, are a mommy, and mommies have the superhero power ability to tune shit out. This is why when I'm standing in line at the bagel place and my kid says, "Mommy Mommy Mommy Mommy Mommy Mommy Mommy Mommy," the bagel lady is like, "Hellllllllo, are you going to answer your child?" And I'm like, "Lady, I'm basically deaf until he says it at least sixteen times." It's an amazing superpower ability, but it totally screws the people around you if you're not careful with it. Muhahahahaha, be careful with your strength, oh powerful one.

So in conclusion, yes, get out your iPads, your iPhones, your LeapPads, your other tablets that I don't know the names of, etc., etc., etc., and use them so you can stay sane and not kill your children or yourself, but try to be responsible about it. The world already hates parents of young children enough.

When I tell my son he can't watch any more TV because he's had enough screen time already, I can't help but feel doubly victorious. Not only is he not zoned out in front of some stupid show, but he also gets tons of exercise by flailing about and throwing a tantrum.

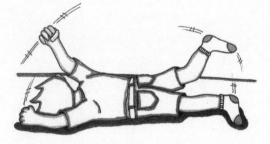

All in favor of feeding rat poison to Chuck E. Cheese, say aye!!

ZOEY: Ewwww, I HATE Barbies!! Let's play fairies.

ELSA: No, I HATE fairies. I wanna play house.

ZOEY: House is for babies.

ELSA: Is not!

ZOEY: Is too!!

I mean seriously, you guys are both wrong. All of those games are stupid and boring as shit and if I wanted to listen to two crotchmuffins fight all day, I would just have Zoey hang out with her brother and I wouldn't have offered to host a playdate. But Elsa's mom isn't coming back to pick her up for three hours, so I have to figure out something that'll make them both happy.

ME: Who wants to go to Chuck E. Cheese?!!

And suddenly they're screaming and screeching and hugging each other like they've been stranded on a desert island and Justin Bieber just pulled up on his yacht without his shirt on.

Now part of me is feeling awesome because I'm about to host the bestest playdate ever, but the other part of me is like, nooooo, WTF were you thinking giving them that option? Because Chuck E. Cheese pretty much sucks more ass than any ass-sucking place there is. And here are seven reasons why:

1. THE TUUUUBE

You know, that gerbil tube that's hanging from the ceiling that the kids are supposed to crawl inside. The way I see it, those tubes are pretty much the CDC without protective clothing and doors that zip closed. I'm like, "Come on kids, take off your shoes, it's time to get Ebola!!" Because do you know what happens inside that tube? A bazillion kids crawl around in there and they all breathe in each other's nasty-ass germs. And I literally mean ASS germs because they're on all fours and everyone has someone else's ass in their face. Until one little douchenugget in there craps his diaper or blows pizza chunks out his pie-hole and the kids all have to make a mad dash for the nearest exit. And God forbid your kid is the wussy who can't figure out how to get out and needs you to come in to rescue him. Whatever you do, no matter how loud he screams, even if he sounds like he's on fire, DO NOT go in there. I'm serious. No kid is worth it. Just call in an Amber Alert and let the police take care of the situation.

2. STUPID, SHITTY GAMES

I mean yeah, a lot of the games at Chuck E. Cheese are fun and cute and take at least 17 seconds to play. And then there's like this whole set of games that you just drop your token in and it rolls down a ramp and IF it lands on the right lily pad you win a ticket or two. But it takes zero skill and you can never hit the right spot and you might as well just put your money into a broken vending machine. I mean seriously, playing these games is like if someone was standing in front of you and every five seconds you just handed them a quarter.

YOU: Here you go . . . 1, 2, 3, 4, 5 . . . here you go . . . 1, 2, 3, 4, 5 . . . here you go . . . 1, 2, 3, 4, 5. . . .

And sixty minutes later, you're out $180. I shit you not, I just did the math. Well, my calculator did. But I had to figure out what numbers to plug into my calculator and holy crap is that hard.

3. FAKE MONEY YOU CAN'T USE ANYWHERE ELSE

Awww shit, like four days after going to Chuck E. Cheese I'm paying for my overpriced mochaccinolatte at the coffee shop and the hipster behind the counter is like, "Uhhhh, we don't take *rat* money," and I see that I've handed him a gold token and I'm mortified. So when I get home, I take all the Chuck E. Cheese tokens out of my wallet and put them in a baggie to save them for the next time we go. And then the next time we go, I'm like, awww shit, I totally forgot to bring our baggie of old tokens. Like seriously, I think I have tokens from 1947.

4. THE RAT

Have you ever wondered how they came up with the Chuck E. Cheese mascot?

FOUNDER: Do you think we should have like a mascot for our restaurant?

OTHER FOUNDER: Yeah. What about a bird?

FOUNDER: Nahh, birds freak me out. A badger?

OTHER FOUNDER: I don't even know WTF a badger is. How about a mouse?

FOUNDER: Hellllllloooo, brainiac, I think a big theme park is already using that one.

OTHER FOUNDER: Okay, fine, what about a rat? A rat is kind of like a mouse.

FOUNDER: A rat, yes! No one's using that. But people don't really like rats in restaurants, do they?

OTHER FOUNDER: Fine, let's just put a bunch of video games in there and then they won't care about the rat.

FOUNDER: Brilliant!

5. **THE TICKETS**

"Hey, kids, time to go!!! Let's cash in our tickets." And then I watch them count out their tickets and one kid has 24 and the other kid has 89. Awesome, this is going to go over well.

KIDDO: How come she has so many?

ME: Because she's really good at games and you suck ass. Now let's go get her a bunch of cool prizes and see if you can afford anything.

6. THE SALAD BAR

Wait a second, did you forget to pick up your free Ebola in the gerbil tube? Awww, no worries, because you can just grab it from the salad bar. I mean seriously? Who the F decided to put a *salad bar* in this place? Ooooh, here's an idea. After everyone has touched joysticks and Skee-Balls and other things that are covered in boogers and never get cleaned, let's have them grab utensils and serve themselves fresh veggies from communal bins. Mmmmm, baby tomatoes with tuberculosis. Deeelish.

7. CASHING IN YOUR TICKETS

KID: Oooh, oooh, I want that SpongeBob toy!

ME: You need one thousand tickets for that.

KID: How many do I have?

ME: Twenty-four.

KID: Can I get that bouncy ball?

ME: You need five hundred tickets for that.

KID: How many do I have?

ME: Twenty-four.

KID: How about that map?

ME: Two hundred and fifty. You have twenty-four. Look in that case down below.

KID: What can I get for twenty-four tickets?

ME: A Tootsie Roll and a plastic lizard.

KID: Wahhh, I don't want a plastic lizard.

ME: Fine, two Tootsie Rolls.

KID: Can I get a whistle?

ME: *(faking disappointment)* Oh nooo, I'm so sorry, but you need twenty-*FIVE* tickets to get an annoying whistle that will make me want to chop my ears off.

PIMPLY KID BEHIND THE COUNTER: It's okay, I'll give her a whistle for twenty-four tickets.

ME: *(through gritted teeth)* Yo dumbass, shut the F up.

KID: Yayyyyyy!!! Can I get it?!

ME: If you're taking public transportation home and not driving home with me.

(Cut to 20 minutes later.)

KID: WOOOOOOOO!!! WOOOOOOOOOOOOOOO!!!! WOOOO OOOOOOOOO!!!!!!

ME: I HATE you, Chuck E. Cheese.

One kid wanted to watch Cars *and the other wanted to watch* Cinderella.

So we're watching Days of Our Lives.

Gag me with a
5-Minute Spider-Man Story

HOLDEN: Mommy, I want this one.

ME: Noooooo, pleeeease don't make me read *5-Minute Spider-Man Stories* again. For the love of God, it will kill me!!!

How did Jesus die? He was crucified. How did the dinosaurs die? An asteroid. How did all the mothers die? They died of boredom when their kids made them read *5-Minute Spider-Man Stories* AGAIN. Seriously, have you ever opened this book? It's like one painstaking story after another of Spider-Man battling some stupid villain and it's poorly written (even shittier than my writing). Oh, and here's the stupidest thing of all about it. Even though every story is only five minutes long, every story ends on the left page, and the next story starts on the right page, so whenever you finish a chapter, your kid can see the next chapter and FA-REAKS out because he wants you to read it NOWWWW!!!! So it's not *5-Minute Spider-Man Stories*. It's *TWENTY-Minute Spider-Man Stories* because you have to read a bunch of them.

And FYI, *5-Minute Spider-Man Stories* is not the only torturous book like this. They make a shitload of these five-minute books, like *5-Minute Princess Stories* and *5-Minute Bible Stories* and *5-Minute Snuggle Stories*, and no, I didn't make that last one up. That is what it's called. Seriously. What it really should be called is *5-Minute Stories That Make Mom Want to Stab Her Eyes Out with an Ice Pick* because then she wouldn't have to read it because she would be blind and they don't make these stupid books in braille. Or maybe they do, which would be totally wrong because isn't life hard enough already being blind? But I digress.

Anyways, I'm putting the kids to bed and it's Holden's turn to pick a book and, of course, this is the shit he picks out. So I make him an offer.

ME: Buddy, instead of reading this, what if I tell you guys a story you've never heard before?

BOTH KIDS: What is it?

ME: It's good. I promise *(even though I have no F'ing idea what it's gonna be)*.

And they reluctantly agree to it.

ME: Okay. Once upon a time there was this really fun boy who lived in a house and one night there were some strange noises outside. He went outside to investigate and he found a weird creature in their shed, so he put out a trail of Reese's Pieces and the creature started eating the candy and came out. That's when the boy found out it wasn't a creature. It was an alien!! And even though the boy was scared, he found out the alien was actually really nice, so he let the alien come live in his house, until one day some bad men wanted to catch the alien. The boy and his big brother got on their bikes and they put the alien in a little basket on the front of the bike and they rode as fast as they could to the forest and the alien's family came down in a spaceship to save him and take him back home to their planet. The boy and the alien were very sad to say good-bye, but they gave each other a big hug and said they would remember each other forever and ever. The End.

ZOEY: That was cool!!

HOLDEN: Yeah!!! What color was the spaceship?

ME: Silver.

ZOEY: ANOTHER STORY! ANOTHER!!

Hells yeah! (a) I F'ing rock, and (b) I didn't have to read any of that five-minute story crap. Because here's the thing. If your kids are all like, "Tell us a story! Tell us a story," all you have to do is tell them the plot of a movie from the 1980s. Seriously, all 1980s movies are awesome for this. Try it.

The Breakfast Club: Once upon a time there were five kids who got in trouble and had to have a time-out all day long . . .

The Karate Kid: Once upon a time there was a boy who didn't have any friends except for this old man who could catch flies with chopsticks . . .

Can't Buy Me Love: Once upon a time there was a girl who was wearing a white dress but her friend accidentally spilled grape juice all over it . . .

Sixteen Candles: Once upon a time there was a girl and it was her birthday but everyone forgot except for one really nice boy at school . . .

Coming to America: Once upon a time there was a prince in Africa and he came all the way to America to find his true love and he found her at McDonald's . . .

Footloose: Once upon a time there was a boy who lived in a town where it was against the law to dance . . .

See? I could go on and on. The plots are simple but creative, and the characters are awesome. So there you go. The next time your kid asks you to read some annoying book, or the next time you're stuck on a long car ride and you don't want to stop and look at the giantest ball of string or play another riveting game of I Spy, or the next time you end up waiting in the doctor's office for nine million minutes until you wonder whether they forgot about you, just reach into your radical brain for your most totally tubular, awesome 1980s movie. You're welcome.

Awww, the kids are playing massage parlor with their stuffed animals. How cute!! Oh, and in case you're wondering what they're using to give massages, let's just say it came out of my nightstand drawer. Bzzzzzzz. Awesome.

ME: *Zoey, if you ask me to play with the iPhone ONE MORE TIME this morning, you're not going to be allowed to play on it for the rest of the day.*

ZOEY: *Mom—*

ME: *Think about what you're about to say.*

ZOEY: *Can I play with the iPAD?*

MY HUBBY IS AWESOME

(But Not as Awesome as Me)

DO I LOVE MY HUBBY? MORE THAN ANYONE ON earth (yes, even Channing Tatum, but don't tell Channing I said that just in case he decides to divorce Jenna and marry me). But there are days I'm like, aggghhhhhh, why can't my hubby do as good a job as me?!! Think, damn it. Multitask, damn it. How hard is it to get the kids dressed BEFORE they come down for breakfast? I mean don't get me wrong, my hubby's super amazing at doing lots of shit. Like tossing our kiddos around like beanbags, teaching them how to burp and fart in the bathtub, and riling them up before bedtime. So F'ing helpful.

P.S. HONEY, IF YOU'RE READING THIS, PLEASE SKIP THIS section. Because I'm about to rag on you. A lot. And to all the other daddies out there reading this, I'm sure none of this applies to you. Right, mommies? Wink, wink.

What you should REALLY F'ing look for in a husband

BACK IN THE DAY before my under-eyes looked like they were made of elephant skin and my vajayjay actually did its job and held shit in (yeah, I'm talkin' to you, 'gina), I used to dream about my future hubby. I used to say shit like, "Mostly I want to find a man who's funny and makes me laugh." But now that I have kids, I'm like screw that. Laughter is so overrated. Because if you're still single, here are some things you're really gonna want in your future baby daddy.

1. Pick someone who's a light sleeper, so when your little crotch-muffin is screaming in the middle of the night, your better half isn't going to be your shittier half snoring away in lalaland while you haul your ass out of bed every time.

2. You want someone who can carry a SHITLOAD of crap. So when you're traveling somewhere, he can carry the suitcase, the car seat, the stroller, the backpacks, the diaper bag, the lunches, and the coats. You know, while you're busy chasing your little douchenugget through the airport to catch him before he boards a plane to Syria.

3. Find someone who's handy and can put shit together. Because yeah, it's awesome that your crib from IKEA only costs $12 and comes in a shoebox, but when the hubby unfolds the instructions and they're in 270 different languages and come with a baggie filled with 7,000 screws, the last thing you need is for him to have a heart attack. Because if he's in the hospital, then guess who's putting that shit together? You.

4. Find a guy who likes to ride amusement park rides, especially the kind that spin around and around and around. That way you can stand off to the side taking beautiful blurry pictures of your hubby and kiddos instead of riding it yourself and projectile vomiting, after which the vomit will sit there in midair until you spin around and it slams you in the face.

5. Pick a guy who's taller than you. Then you can store lots of stuff up high in the house and use it as an excuse to make him do shit that you don't want to do. "Oh honey, I'd totally change his urine-soaked sheets at 3 a.m., but I can't reach his clean bedding, and it doesn't make sense for *both* of us to get up. Guess I'll have to keep lying here all snug in this comforter while you do it."

6. But seriously, who gives a shit who you fall in love with? If he doesn't come with good parents, ditch him. Because good in-laws are great for all sorts of things. Like buying shoes and underwear for your kids when they grow out of them every week, and babysitting, and leaving right after babysitting so you don't have to stand there and chitchat at the end of the night pretending like you're sober.

7. Look for a guy who's kinda dirty. That's right, if you walk into his super-fugly bachelor pad and you squat over the toilet because you're afraid, you just found yourself a winner. Because guess who's NOT going to bitch at you for leaving the macaroni and cheese pot soaking in the sink for three days. Mr. McGrossy.

8. Find a total pussy. Nahhh, I don't mean become a lesbian. Well, unless you want to become a lesbian. Then become a lesbian. But if you're looking for a dude, find a dude who's a total pussy. Because macho dudes won't change diapers. And macho dudes won't drive a minivan. And macho dudes won't hold your purse when you go into a porta-potty.

9. Find a guy who can blow his load in less than three minutes. Because when you're trying to get preggers again and he's jackhammering away at you while your firstborn is body-slamming your bedroom door trying to break it down scream-ing, "WHY IS IT LOCKED??!!!" you just want to get shit done as fast as possible.

10. Find someone who's gonna make you laugh. 'Cause you will never need a sense of humor more than you do once you have kids.

ZOEY: *Mommy, my bagina itches.*

ME: *Your what?*

ZOEY: *My bagina.*

ME: *Your VAgina. Va. Va.*

ZOEY: *My VAgina.*

ME: *Yes, and actually it's your vulva.*

ZOEY: *I have a vulda?*

ME: *A vulVA. Va. Va.*

HUBBY: *(interrupting) What the HELL is a vulva?*

ME: *It's like that whole area down there.*

HUBBY: *All I know is the clit.*

Sometimes I feel like I'm the only parent in this house. Ya know?

Men are from Mars, where apparently they don't make PB&Js

SO THIS MORNING I HAD TO MAKE an important phone call, so I asked my hubby to get the kiddos dressed and to pack the PB&Js for our day at the zoo. Forty minutes later, I came into the kitchen and the kids were still in their jammies and my hubby was STILL making the sandwiches. I'm like WTF have you been doing all this time? And then I saw.

This is how a mom makes six PB&Js:

Take out twelve pieces of bread

Quickly spread peanut butter on six of them

Quickly spread jelly on the other six

Slap them together and shove them into bags

And this is how a dad does it:

Take out one piece of bread

Put peanut butter on it

Make sure the peanut butter is evenly spread all the way to the edges

Take out another piece of bread

Wipe the knife off

Put jelly on the bread

Close the sandwich

Wipe the knife off

Cut the sandwich in half

Go get a baggie

Carefully put the sandwich into the baggie

Take out one piece of bread

Put peanut butter on it

Make sure the peanut butter is evenly spread all the way to the edges

Take out another piece of bread

Wipe the knife off

Put jelly on the bread

Close the sandwich

Wipe the knife off

Cut the sandwich in half

Go get a baggie

Carefully put the sandwich into the baggie

Take out one piece of bread

Put peanut butter on it

Make sure the peanut butter is evenly spread all the way to the edges

Take out another piece of bread

Wipe the knife off

Put jelly on the bread

Close the sandwich

Wipe the knife off

Cut the sandwich in half

Go get a baggie

Carefully put the sandwich into the baggie

Take out one piece of bread

Put peanut butter on it

Make sure the peanut butter is evenly spread all the way to the edges

Take out another piece of bread

Wipe the knife off

Put jelly on the bread

Close the sandwich

Wipe the knife off

Cut the sandwich in half

Go get a baggie

Carefully put the sandwich into the baggie

Take out one piece of bread

Put peanut butter on it

Make sure the peanut butter is evenly spread all the way to the edges

Take out another piece of bread

Wipe the knife off

Put jelly on the bread

Close the sandwich

Wipe the knife off

Cut the sandwich in half

Go get a baggie

Carefully put the sandwich into the baggie

Take out one piece of bread

Put peanut butter on it

Make sure the peanut butter is evenly spread all the way to the edges

Take out another piece of bread

Wipe the knife off

Put jelly on the bread

Close the sandwich

Wipe the knife off

Cut the sandwich in half

Go get a baggie

Carefully put the sandwich into the baggie

So by all means, if you are not eating lunch until 6 p.m., ask your husband to make it.

HOLDEN: *Where is Daddy?*

ME: *Where do you think Daddy is?*

HOLDEN: *Him died.*

(I call my husband on my cell phone.)

DADDY: *Hey, what's up?*

ME: *Just checking. See you at dinner tonight.*

(click)

A bunch of shit my hubby
does better than me

YO GOD, LEMME GET THIS STRAIGHT. If I want to make a baby, I need a man. Like if I want to make a real live human being with organs and a brain and a central nervous system and complicated shit like that, I need a guy to do it. But if I want to make something super simple, like a sandwich or a bed, having a guy there to help me is actually a liability. How does that make sense? Like the other day I asked my hubby to make Zoey's bed and he tucked the blanket like four feet under the foot of the bed so now if she wants covers she has to sleep halfway down her mattress every night. I mean sure, I could remake it and pull the blanket up higher, but I'm lazy, so I'll just fix it when I change the sheets in a few weeks, uhhh, I mean days. Someone please explain to me why men cannot complete some of the simplest tasks on this planet.

Yup, I rag on my hubby all the time for the shit he can't do as well as me. Bwhahahaha, you call THAT a ponytail?!!! Bwhahahaha, all of your white socks are pink now! Bwhahahaha, is this a hamburger or a hockey puck? Of course, I'm sure there's a bunch of shit he could make fun of me for, but he doesn't because he's way more mature than I am. And because he knows I'll kick his ass if he does. Like how I can't catch a ball to save my life. Or how I would have no idea how to clean the gutters. Or how I can't reach the vitamins in our cabinets because I'm short and since I'm usually too lazy to drag a chair over, I end up jumping and missing and jumping and missing and jumping and missing until I finally manage to knock the bottle over with my finger and it rolls out and I catch it and then I turn around and he's staring at me like I'm a crazy person.

Anyways, the truth is, we both suck at lots of shit and we're both awesome at lots of shit. But the good news is that it's different shit. Which is why we work so well together. He's my better half and I'm his better half, so together we make one decent human being. Which leads me to my point. Yes, I actually have a point.

Dear Hubby,

Here's a list of stuff you do better than me. And no, I was not abducted by aliens, and yes, this is actually me typing this.

1. *You don't multitask. Now I know what you're thinking. WTF kind of backhanded compliment is that? But seriously, this is a good thing. You know how I'm constantly doing two things at once? Playing with the kids and checking my email, doing an art project with the kids and making dinner, watching a movie with the kids and folding laundry. I am never fully there with them. You, on the other hand, can't do two things at once*

so if you're hanging out with the kids, you are hanging out with the kids. And they have 100% of your attention and they love you for it.

2. *Okay, here's how I give the kids a bath.*

    ME: Honeyyy, can you give the kids a bath?!!!

    Seriously. You give the kids a bath every night so when I try to do it, Zoey screams and yells like her eyes are on fire when I wash the shampoo out because apparently I can't shield her face from the water like you do. Or I get them out of the tub and they yell at me because I don't wrap them up like burritos the same way you do. Ooooh, excuuuse me for doing it all Chipotle-style and not Taco Bell–style or however the hell Daddy does it.

3. *If one of the kids jumps on my back, I'm like, "Yo douchenugget, if you EVER jump on me like that again, I am going to elbow you in the face and ground you forever." But you, dear hubby, actually get on all fours and beg them to climb aboard. And then you gallop across the playroom and let them kick you over and over again in the nuts and jump on your head and shit.*

4. **HUBBY:** Holden, put your shoes on. Holden, please put your shoes on. Holden, put your shoes on. Holden, can you put your shoes on, please? Holden, it's time for your shoes. Holden, your shoes. Holden, put your shoes on.

    Times like a million until he finally stops whatever he's doing and comes over to put his shoes on. You have the patience of an F'ing statue getting shat on by a pigeon. Unlike me, who has this little tiny switch that flips whenever I have to tell the kids more than three times to put their shoes on, at which time I go BALLISTIC and turn into a verbally abusive Tasmanian devil.

5. *And, of course, last but not least, taking out the trash, cleaning the gutters, telling me to quit buying shit we don't need, getting dingleberries off the cat, paying the utility bills, giving me cash because I never have any, standing in line at the cash register so I can keep shopping, carrying shit down to the basement, setting mousetraps, coming quickly when I'm screaming, emptying mousetraps, being our airport pack mule, moving the car seat because I have no F'ing clue how to, etc., etc., etc., etc.*

> *Love,*
> *The woman who acts like she could do it all without you, even though there's no F'ing way she could*

P.S. FYI, there are way more than five things I can put on this list, but I'm lazy and if I write too many I'm afraid it will go to your head.

HUSBAND: *Why do we always have to do it in the dark now?*

ME: *Not true, I can see you in the glow of the video monitor.*

Et ee um a-er owls

HOLDEN: Mommy?

DADDY: Holden, go back to bed.

HOLDEN: No, Daddy, I don't want youuuu. I want Mommm-mmmy.

ME: Holden, listen to your dad. It's only 5:20, go back to bed.

HOLDEN: Nooooooo. I wanna sleep with you.

ME: Fine, but you have to really sleep and you can't talk.

HOLDEN: Mommy, face me.

ME: No, I'm facing this way right now.

HOLDEN: No, Mommmmmy, FACE me!!!

ME: Fine.

So I roll over so we're lying on our sides and our heads are on the same pillow, face-to-face.

HOLDEN: Mommy.

ME: No talking. Sleep.

HOLDEN: But Mommy.

ME: WHAT Holden?

HOLDEN: *BARRRRRRFFFFFFFFFFFFFFFF!!!!!!*

I shit you not. It was like he stopped at the all-you-can-eat buffet on the way to our bedroom and then decided my face was the all-you-can-vomit receptacle.

DADDY: Oh my God.

ME: *(through gritted teeth)* Et ee um a-er owls.

DADDY: What?

ME: *(through gritted teeth)* Et ee um a-er owls.

TRANSLATION: Get me some paper towels.

REAL TRANSLATION: Why the F are you still standing there? You better sprint as fast as humanly possible to the kitchen and get me some F'ing paper towels in the next two seconds or puke is going to seep into my mouth and then I'm gonna throw up too and you're gonna be up to your elbows in Pukesville cleaning this shit up without me and then we are getting divorced.

Seriously, this is the shit they mean when they say in sickness and in health.

DADDY: Oh, buddy, are you okay? Is it your tummy?

Are you kidding me? Is *HE* okay?!!! He's fine. He just threw up so he probably feels a little better now. I'll tell you who is NOT okay. The woman who was literally 6 inches away from his mouth when it decided to turn into an explosive cannon and projectile vomit at 60 miles per hour into five of her open orifices.

DADDY: Do you want a sip of water, buddy?

ME: AGGGHHHHHHH!!!

Only it comes out as "MMMMGGGHHHHHH!!!" because I still can't open my mouth because it's basically wired shut until someone gets me some F'ing paper towels. He finally gets the message and heads out of the room and God help him if he comes back with Holden's toothbrush and toothpaste and doesn't come back with something to clean me off.

Luckily for him, he returns holding some paper towels. TWO of them. Are you shitting me? I mean it takes more effort to tear off two paper towels than it does to bring the whole roll.

DADDY: I grabbed them as fast as I could.

He hands me them, I wipe off my face, and as soon as I'm 200% sure that no throw-up is going to leak into my mouth, I speak.

ME: I will now be getting into the shower and standing under scalding-hot water for the next 30 minutes. And then I will be headed to Atlanta to go to the CDC to get decontaminated. Take care of everything without me. I'll be back in time for dinner. Not to cook it. To eat it.

Look, my hubby wrapped a present for me! Eeeeeks, I wonder what it is!! Do you think it's the bracelet I asked for from Tiffany?!

Why I stopped liking sex (Grandma, please don't read this chapter)

I DON'T LIKE SEX. Not anymore. I mean I used to lovvvve sex but it's kind of impossible to like it after you've been forced to have it for eight months straight over and over and over again. You see, after I was kidnapped by a ring of whip-yielding pimps, nahhhh, just kidding. Sorry. Seriously, sorrrrry. I totally shouldn't joke about pimps and sex slavery and shit. That stuff is real and horrible and no one should be forced to share their body with anyone, so that was a bad joke. But I'm not joking about sex.

I know what some of you are thinking. "Boo-hoo-hooo, that's so sad that you don't love sex anymore. I feel so bad for you and your cold vagina. Maybe you should just try having more sex? My hugglepoo and I do it every single night and sometimes even twice when we're feeling frisky."

Well, (a) I wouldn't want to be like you because you use annoying words like *frisky*, and (b) come tell me that after you HAVE TO have sex a lot for eight months straight.

Okay, lemme explain. It all started when I was twenty-nine.

Aggghhhh, why haven't I met my husband yet?!! The plan was to meet him by the time I was twenty-five. I mean really I thought I was gonna marry my high school boyfriend, and then I thought I was gonna marry my second high school boyfriend, and then my third high school boyfriend, and then a few more, and then a few my freshman year in college, etc., etc., etc., all the way until I was twenty-five when I was dating this total asswipe who I kept thinking would change into the perfect prince the way asswipes often do in the movies so I could marry him. But nope, out of 247 boyfriends between the ages of fifteen and twenty-nine, not a single one panned out. Shit.

And then when I was twenty-nine, I met the man of my dreams. The man of my desperate twenty-nine-year-old dreams who actually sucked and it took me four and a half lonnnnnng wasted years to figure out that our relationship was like two puzzle pieces you keep trying to jam together even though they don't F'ing fit but they're the only two puzzle pieces left because you don't realize that you accidentally left another piece in the box. But as I was desperately clinging on to the relationship in hopes that it would work because I couldn't find the right puzzle piece, the eggs in my ovaries were getting older and wrinkly and growing wiry gray hairs.

ME: I don't know, Doc, I just keep hearing this loud ticking noise in my ears.

DOCTOR: That's your biological clock ticking. It gets louder the closer you get to becoming an old childless hag.

I mean now that I have kids, I actually recognize that childless people have totally AWESOME lives that are often better than those of us who are parents, but at the time I thought my life would be over if I didn't get to have children. I was hunting for a husband like I was fighting for my life in the Hunger Games.

And then when I was thirty-four, I met him. And no, it didn't happen when I least expected it to like all those jackasses say it will. I worked my ass off to find the right guy. I was on multiple dating websites forcing myself to go on at least one date every week, and going way out of my comfort zone, saying yes to pretty much anyone, including men with receding hairlines who wore black pants with brown belts and gross tank tops. Yup, I lowered my bar in the clothing department and raised my bar in the personality department, and I found the man of my dreams. The *REAL* man of my dreams. And we had great sex. Lots of it. And it was AWESOMMMMMME. And we both wanted to get married and we both wanted to have kiddos and we both knew that my eggs were slowly rolling toward the assisted living facility for senior citizen eggs, so we didn't waste any time.

ME: We should probably start trying to have a baby right away because it might take a while.

HIM: Yes. Me want sex.

And guess what!? We were preggers within two short months!! I don't know what everyone's talking about, it's so easy getting pregnant (FYI, I'm not this big of a douchebag. Keep reading).

And then we had Zoey and life was awesome, even though we never slept and we couldn't go out anymore and my boobs were more hangy than my uvula and none of my pants fit, etc., etc., etc. But still, everything was great and we knew we wanted to have a second.

HIM: We should have another so they can play together and make things easier.

ME: Definitely.

PEOPLE WHO ALREADY HAVE MORE THAN ONE CHILD: Bwhahaha-hahahahahaha!!!!

At my hubby's suggestion, we started trying right away.

ME: But I'm not even ovulating right now.

HIM: You might be. We should have sex just in case.

And when I got my period that first month, I wasn't surprised. Disappointed? Maybe a little. But not discouraged. I mean this was exactly what happened the first time. And I fully expected to be pregnant by month two.

Then month two came and I remember sitting at my desk and feeling a little pain in my belly. OMGeeeee, is that the embryo implanting?!!! I was super excited. And then a few hours later I felt it again. That embryo must really be burrowing into that lining. And then by that evening I was spotting a little. Eeeeeeks, it's happening!!! And then by the next morning I was digging through every old purse in my closet to find a tampon because I hadn't bought a new box of them because I fully expected to be preggers this month and hell if I was gonna spend a bunch of money on tampons I didn't need. Shit. Now I was disappointed.

ME: I'm not pregnant.

HIM: Good. Me want more sex.

So the first thing I did was go to Costco and buy a GIANT box of tampons because Murphy's Law says the bigger the box I buy, the faster I will get pregnant. And then I went to the Internet and started to research ovulation calculators. It was asking me things like dates and cycle length and luteal phase and I'm like WTH does the moon have to do with it? And since my cycle wasn't always regular, I figured out that I was gonna be fertile sometime between June 4th and June 10th and that we should have sex every *other* day because that would give my hubby time to replenish his sperm supply (apparently sperm need time to reproduce too).

So we waited. And waited. Until . . .

ME: Honey, we need to have sex today!!

And his clothes were off before I had even finished saying the word *today*. And then after we were done, I laid there. No wait, I just got laid. I lied there. Or did I lay there? Whatever, I reclined there on my back visualizing all the little spermies racing to the egg to see who would get there first. It was so exciting to think about them nibbling away to fertilize the egg or however they do it. And then, exactly forty-eight hours later, doo da doo da doo doo doo. Doo da doo da doo doo doo.

HIM: What is that noise?

ME: Oh, that's my alarm. Time to have sex!

Yup, I set an alarm to remind us. So we did it. And forty-eight hours after that. Doo da doo da doo doo doo. Doo da doo da doo doo doo.

HIM: Again?

Neither of us was really in the mood, but it was time so we did it again. Phew, three times in one week. We're definitely going to be pregnant now!!

UTERUS: Fuck you!!!! You're not in charge here!

Yup, Aunt Flo arrived again. So every month we kept trying. Insert, repeat, insert, repeat, insert, repeat, over and over again until my vagina felt like someone had put one of those medieval torture devices in it that looks like an umbrella that they open up inside you and my hubby's peeper felt like someone had rubbed it against a cheese grater for a couple of hours to make shredded penis. Mmmm, a delicacy in many countries.

Okay, now close your eyes because I want you to picture something. Awww shit, you can't read with your eyes closed. Fine, open them back up and close them figuratively. Now picture me and my husband having sex. Agghhh, nooo, you're blind now!!! I totally apologize. My bad. So don't actually picture *us*. Picture my head on Gisele's body and my hubby's head on Channing Tatum's body and now picture us having sex. There, that's better. So now what I want you to do is picture Harry Potter standing next to the bed while we're having sex and he's pointing his totally powerful wand at us and he is literally sucking alllllll the magic out of our sex. It's like electric lightning is shooting out of our naked bodies and it's all being sucked into his wand. And when he's all done, he vanishes into a puff of smoke and we are left there still doing it. Not making passionate love. Not getting it on. Not fucking. Just doing it. In out in out in out in out.

Because that's what sex had become for us. Something we had to do. A chore.

HIM: We need more lube. Here is the bottle.

ME: Okay, it's applied.

HIM: That's good. I'm going to cum.

ME: It's about time.

HIM: All done.

ME: Okay, I'll lie here for the next forty-eight hours and then come back so we can do it again.

It was about as enjoyable as putting together Zoey's new bike. But worse because imagine putting that bike together over and over again, three or four times a week every month, but then the next morning you wake up and there's no bike. Shit, does that analogy even make sense? I don't know, but basically all I'm saying is that when you *have to* have sex many, many times, it starts to become a chore.

And every month I would be somewhere when I would feel the first twinge of cramping and I would kid myself into thinking it wasn't period cramps, and that maybe I just had to poop or something. And then as the day went on the pains would get stronger and all I could think about was nooooo, I don't want to have to have sex anymore. I mean don't get me wrong, I love my husband to death and I think he's crazy sexy, but I just didn't want to do it anymore. And I wasn't alone. He was pretty much over the whole sex thing too. And let me tell you this, if your husband doesn't want sex anymore, something is wrong.

We felt annoyed, irritable, angry, guilty, exhausted, and spent. These are all really great things for a marriage, by the way.

Anyways, this went on for eight months. Eight lonnnnnnng months of doing it and doing it and doing it without the result we wanted. And pleeeease don't think I'm an asshole for complaining about eight months when there are so many couples out there who do it for years without conceiving and who have to get shots and pay shitloads of money and buy eggs and feel those awful cramps month after month after month for years on end. If eight months was bad for us, I can't imagine what it's like for some couples and my heart goes out to them. Big time.

And then one day I didn't get the twinge of pain, so I peed on a stick and there it was. Clear as day. The blue line. I wanted to jump for joy but I didn't because I was too scared I would dislodge the baby.

ME: Honey, guess what? We're pregnant.

HIM: Really? We did it?!!

ME: We did it.

Yup, we did it. A LOT. But it finally worked. I don't know which we were more excited about. The fact that we were pregnant or the fact that we didn't have to have sex anymore. Until after the baby arrived and we got the green light from the gynie.

GYNIE: Well, it's been six weeks. You can have sex again.

ME: Do we have to?

I mean no, I didn't really say that out loud. And I'm happy to say this isn't the end to our story. Because guess who showed up to our bed again one day! Harry Potter!!! Completely out of the blue! Yup, one day he randomly showed up and he aimed that magic wand at us and zappppppp, he gave us back our sex magic!!! Needless to say, my hubby was a little perplexed when I started yelling, "Thank you, Harry!!!" in the middle of our sexcapade, but at least the magic was back. Phew.

And now my hubby won't stop asking for it again. Everything's back to normal.

HOLDEN: *I want a cup.*

HUBBY: *Where are the cups?*

ME: *Where the cups are.*

I mean seriously? Did we seriously need to have this conversation? Does anyone else out there deal with this shit?

You didn't think I'd just write a chapter about all the shit he does right, did you?

Dear Schmoopie Woopie,

I love you. Wait, I mean I LOVVVVVVVVVVVVVE you. Like when you kiss me, I still get those butterflies in my belly, and when you wash that pot that's been "soaking" in the sink for 48 hours, I get weak in the knees. But here's the thing. I would really, really be appreciative (yes, THAT kind of appreciative) if you would stop doing a few annoying things:

1. Stop asking me stupid shit. I'm not saying you're stupid. In fact, I'm saying you're pretty F'ing intelligent, so stop asking me stupid shit like "Do we have more milk?" Ummmm, hello brainiac, open the fridge and look. Heyyyy, look at that, milk! Who'da thunk it'd be in the fridge?!

2. Step one: Take off your dirty clothes.

Step two: Look in the mirror and say something cheesy like "Holy crap, there's a hot naked guy in this mirror!"

Step three: Throw your dirty clothes in the hamper. Not ON the hamper. IN the hamper. I mean seriously, is it that hard to pick up the lid? It weighs less than the beer you pick up every night.

3. *You know what drives me BONNNN-NNKERS?! When I'm literally un-packing bags of groceries I just bought and you say something like "Oh yeah, we ran out of apple juice this morning." I'm like WTF WTF WTF??? "Why didn't you write it on the list?!" So whatta you do? You walk over to the list and write apple juice on it. My nice, clean list that has nothing on it because I JUST WENT SHOPPING!!!*

4A. *Okay, so when I offer to wash the dishes after dinner, here's what I want you to do. Don't help me. Don't hang out in the kitchen. Don't "keep me company." Pick up both kiddos and get the F out of there. And don't feel guilty about it. When I say I WANT to wash the dishes, what I'm really saying is that I'll stand at the sink and scrub dried cheese off plates if that's what it takes to be completely alone with a glass of vino. Capeesh?*

4B. *And if you accidentally forget 4A, please don't come up behind me at the sink and try to put your you-know-what in my ba-donkadonk. Yeah, I'm psyched you still think I'm sexy, but the kids are still awake right now and probably doing something annoying like drawing on my walls or putting holes in them or rifling through my nightstand drawer. So the last thing I want to do at the moment is procreate.*

5. *ME: Can we throw that shirt out, pleeeeease? Look at the pit stains.*

   YOU: Are you kidding? I've had this shirt since high school!

   Bwhahahahha, I think it's F'ing HYSTERICAL that you think this is a selling point. Ohhh yeah, how could you ever throw out a shirt that you've been sweating in for twenty-two years?

6. *Honey, you know we're getting off at the next exit, right? Honey, we need to get off at the next exit. Honey, our exit is in a quarter of a mile. HONEY, GET THE F OVER NOWWWWW BECAUSE IF YOU WAIT WE'RE EITHER GOING TO MISS OUR EXIT OR WE'RE GOING TO HIT THAT GIANT 18-WHEELER AND WE'RE ALL GOING TO DIE!!! So whether I'm saying these things in my head or whether I can't help myself and I'm saying them out loud, WHYYYY??? WHY do you insist on driving in the left-hand lane until like a split second before we need to get off the highway? We're either going to die when we slam into a giant Mack truck or I'm going to die from an F'ing heart attack.*

7. *If you are wearing black pants, don't wear brown shoes. If you are wearing brown pants, don't wear black shoes. If you are wearing black socks, make sure they are the same black. Holes in old boxer shorts do not make you comfy, they make you an exhibitionist. Holes in old jeans do not make you comfy, they make you look like you traveled here in a time machine from the 1980s. Oh and please, whatever you do, do NOT wear that braided maroon, navy, and tan belt anymore. You're lucky I don't know where you got it because I am not a violent person, but if I knew I would go there and hunt down and brutally murder the person who sold it to you.*

So there you go. And I know what you're gonna say. You're gonna say that I shouldn't talk because I do some annoying crap too. Like my nagging. Well, if I'm nagging, it means you're doing something wrong. Like something on this list. So just stop doing it, and I'll stop nagging you. Simple as that.

xoxoxoxoxoxoxoxoxoxoxoxoxoxoxoxoxoxoxo,
Your honey bunny

ME: *Honey, can you get the Push-Ups for the kids?*

HUBBY: *Sure. Where are they?*

ME: *In the downstairs freezer.*

(He comes back up three minutes later.)

HUBBY: *I can't find them. Are you sure they're there?*

ME: *200% sure because I checked before the BBQ to make sure we had enough.*

(He comes back up two minutes later.)

HUBBY: *Nope, not there.*

ME: *They are there. Go look again.*

HUBBY: *Are you sure?*

ME: *YES!!*

TEXT FROM HUBBY: *I can't find them.*

TEXT FROM ME: *Keep looking.*

(Two minutes later he comes back up carrying guess what.)

HUBBY: *Got them!*

ME: *Where were they?*

(Because yes, I need him to say it.)

HUBBY: *In the downstairs freezer. I just couldn't find them because the box was turned sideways and I couldn't see the picture of the push-up.*

ME: *I'm sorry, I should have had the picture facing the front. I didn't realize you were illiterate.*

FYI, I did not say this last part out loud. I wanted to, but I restrained myself because I imagine this is the kind of stuff marriage counselors suggest you keep to yourself.

HUBBY: *I don't know which I love more, you or this big deep-dish pizza.*

ME: *I'd like to see that pizza give you a blowjob.*

Teach Your Douchenuggets
to Be Less Douchey and
MORE NUGGETY

HERE ARE A FEW WORDS I CALL KIDS SOMETIMES (and no Mrs. McPerfectpants, I don't say it to their faces): rugrats, douchenuggets, crotchmuffins, a-holios, whinemeisters, sucktots, dicklings, and assbeanies. I mean it's not like kiddos are jerkwads all the time, but oh my gawwwwd are there days that I wish I believed in corporal punishment. Kids love to test their boundaries and break the rules and do all sorts of naughty shit just to see what happens. Wanna know what happens, kiddo? I punish your ass (not literally—see corporal punishment comment up above). But yeah, I'm a bit of a hard-ass. Because guess what cute little a-holes who aren't punished grow up to be. Assholes. Big ones. And we have enough of those on this planet already.

ME: *Zoey, either you stop doing that or I'm going to have to punish you.*

ZOEY: *Like you'll take my Isabelle doll away?*

ME: *Yes, like that.*

ZOEY: *That's okay, I don't care about her anyway.*

ME: *Fine, I'll do something else.*

ZOEY: *Why don't you take my dollhouse away?*

ME: *You never play with that anyway.*

ZOEY: *How about my swing set?*

ME: *Stop saying all the punishments. You don't get to decide.*

ZOEY: *What if I don't get books tonight?*

ME: *Stop it or I'm sending you to bed without dinner.*

ZOEY: *That might be a good one. What are we having?*

Make sure people don't like you for your bagina

OKAY, YOU KNOW WHAT'S TOTALLY AWESOME? When you're invited to hang out at your friend's house for an evening with a bunch of other families and all of the kids are finally old enough to run off and leave you the hell alone so you can actually finish wine and sentences and conversations and not worry too much. Until this happens.

BOY: Miss Karen, the girls just showed us their baginas.

AGGHHHHHH, they showed you WHAT?! I mean yes, I heard him quite clearly the first time, but for some reason my natural reaction was to make him repeat it, which makes absolutely no sense since it was pretty damn painful hearing it once.

BOY: The girls showed us their baginas.

Shiiiiiiiiiit!!!!
My first reaction was to storm into the room where Zoey was and turn into Cujo, but I somehow managed to control my anger and not beat the crap out of her.

ME: *(what I wanted to say)* WTF are you doing???!!! Only slut-bags do that!!

ME: *(what I actually said)* Zoey, come with me into the other room, please. *(walk walk walk)* Why would you show people your vagina?

ZOEY: They said we should.

ME: Who said you should?

ZOEY: *(shrug)* They.

ME: Zoey, you know that's your private part. You don't show that to anyone.

ZOEY: Except you and Daddy and the doctor.

ME: Yes, that's it. *No one* else.

ZOEY: *(truly regretful)* I'm sorry, Mommy.

I gave her a hug and I was about to say, "Go back and play with the other kids, but keep your clothes on," when I realized something. I was letting a good teaching opportunity pass me by. I mean my daughter might not know about the birds and the bees yet, but it's never too early to teach her about self-respect.

ME: Zoey, do you know why people like you?

ZOEY: Because I'm nice.

ME: Yes. And funny and creative and smart and all sorts of other things. Things in here *(I point to her head)* and in here *(I point to her heart)*. People don't like you for your body. They like you for what's INSIDE your body. Understand?

ZOEY: Yes.

And I think she understood. At least at that very moment she did. But I know there are going to be lots of moments in her life that will make this lesson confusing. Like when a boy likes her for her pretty face. Or when she figures out she can get attention by wearing a short skirt. Or when she learns that her body actually has a crapload of power.

So it's my job to teach her that you DON'T share your body to convince someone to like you. That you convince someone to like you and THEN you can share your body if you want. And not until you're older. Much older. Like 147.

And if that doesn't work, then I'll just turn into Cujo and beat the crap out of her.

HOLDEN: *Oh fuck.*

ME: *No, no, nooooo, you do not say that word. Only bad people say that word.*

HOLDEN: *And parents.*

ME: *Yes, and parents.*

I'd totally kick your ass if my toenails weren't still drying

OKAY, SO I TOTALLY KNOW what you're supposed to look like when you greet your hubby at the end of the day. You're supposed to be all fresh and put together, preferably wearing an apron and holding a drink for him in your hand with your luscious lips all

puckered up. Bwahahahahhaha!! 'Cause THIS is how I looked when my hubby walked through the door yesterday.

He took one look at me and said, "What's for dinner?" Nahhh, just kidding. The last time he did that he lost a genital. But seriously, he took one look at me and said, "Rough day?"

ME: The kids are downstairs. Dinner is in the pantry. I'll be back later.

And by *later* I meant whenever the F I want. I didn't tell him where I was going and I didn't wait for an answer. I just grabbed the keys and pulled a Thelma and Louise, minus the whole driving off the cliff part. I mean, WTF, these two women finally learn how to stand up for themselves and what do they do with their freedom? They decide to commit double suicide. Yeah, that's empowering. Not. But I digress. Anyways, I debated where to go:

A. Target, but my legs were killlllling me. Wait, is it okay to ride around on one of those electric cart thingies that has a basket on it if you're not handicapped? Hmmm, probably not.

B. The gym, but that would require belonging to a gym.

C. The nail salon. OMG, yes. Do I care if some stranger is going to see my Chewbacca legs that haven't been shaved all winter? Not. At. All.

So I went in, said I wanted a pedicure, took like 9,000 minutes to figure out which color I wanted because I'd probably be wearing it for the next six months, let the skinny little hairless Asian lady try to pull my very tight leggings up over my elephant calves, and then I finally sat down in the big ole massage chair, where I debated whether I picked the right color but my feet were already in the hot water that was wayyyy too hot and probably scalding me, but I was too embarrassed to say anything.

And then I sat. And sat. And sat. And I closed my eyes, and I relaxed for the first time that day. And even though the massage chair was vibrating and rattling my brain and repeatedly giving me multiple concussions, I didn't give a crap and it was ahhhh-mazing.

And at one point I was tempted to pick up my cell phone and call my friend, but I didn't want to be THAT jackass who ruins the peace and quiet for everyone in there. No way, hozay. Wait, speaking of jackasses, WTF is that sound?

"Wahhhhhhhh!!!!!!!"

I opened my eyes. OMG, you've got to be kidding me.

A mom had just walked in carrying her screaming 2.5-year-old toddler.

Yo lady, it's okay to be five minutes late to your nail appointment because your kid is freaking out and you want to calm her down outside before you bring her inside and bother everyone else.

MOM WHO SUCKS ASS: Come on, sweetie pie, we're here. It's time to get your nails done.

SCREAMING CROTCHMUFFIN: Wahhhhhhhhhhhh!!!!!!!!!!!!!!

Wait, WHAT?!!! She's here to get her 2.5-year-old's nails done? I mean no, I couldn't give a rat's ass if you want to shell out $20 to get your toddler's minuscule nails painted with literally one drop of nail polish on each nail. I've even done it for Zoey on special occasions. But what I could give a rat's ass about is you wanting to get your toddler's nails done so badly that you are willing to do it when she's in the middle of a screaming tantrum and it's ruining the peace and quiet for everyone in the nail salon.

MOM WHO SUCKS ASS: Now stop crying, cutie-wootie. You don't want to bother the other people.

No shit, Sherlock.

MOM WHO SUCKS ASS: Come on, munchkin, what kind of purple do you want?

SCREAMING CROTCHMUFFIN: No purple!!!!

MOM WHO SUCKS ASS: Pink?

SCREAMING CROTCHMUFFIN: No color!!!!!!!

MOM WHO SUCKS ASS: Does that mean clear?

SCREAMING CROTCHMUFFIN: NOOOOOOO COLOR!!!!!

Yo dumbshit, I'm pretty sure what your howler monkey is trying to say is that she doesn't want to get her nails painted. Which is awesome, because nobody else wants her to get her nails painted either. Oh, and here's another good reason. NOT getting your nails painted is free! But nooooo, you've brought your toddler to the nail salon and you aren't leaving until her nails are pink or purple.

MOM WHO SUCKS ASS: I'm sorry, she's just overtired.

Ummm, why is that? Could that be because you've schlepped her to Neimans (Niemans?? Nemans?? Side note, I am so F'ing proud that I don't know how to spell Neimans) and the BMW dealership and your polo lesson and the Evian factory and all the other places you've probably dragged her to all day? I mean no, I didn't know this for sure, but I'll tell you what I did know. When your crotchmuffin is screaming her head off and throwing a mega tantrum, you DO NOT reward her by giving her a $20 manicure. Especially when the other moms in the salon are trying to black out the shit they've gone through that day with their own little hooligans.

MOM WHO SUCKS ASS: Sweetie pie, calm down, you *need* to get your nails done.

Uhhhh, no she doesn't. Kids don't *need* to get their nails done. They need to get their nails clipped. And that's easy. Just pin her to the ground in front of *Caillou* or some other shitty show that hypnotizes children and clip her F'ing nails.

Anyways, luckily the little girl eventually stopped screaming. When she fell asleep sitting in the chair while someone was painting her nails. I shit you not. I can't wait to see what she's like when she grows up. FYI, that's just a saying. Really I pray I never see that little howler monkey ever again. Or her mom, who sucks ass.

ZOEY: *I won the quiet game!*

HOLDEN: *No, I won it!*

ZOEY: *NO, I WON IT!!!!*

HOLDEN: *No, you didn't!!!*

ZOEY: *YES, I DID!!!*

HOLDEN: *NOOO, YOU DIDN'TTTTTT!!!!!*

Well, that worked. Awesome.

Boy, was I wrong

SO I HAVE A CONFESSION TO MAKE. I mean, yeah, my whole life is basically one big confession of alllllllllll the shit I've done wrong, but this is kinda a biggie. You're gonna think I'm a total a-hole for saying this. Okay, deep breath, here it is.

I never wanted to have a boy.

See, you totally think I'm a jerk now, don't you? I mean who the hell says that, only an a-hole, right? All you're supposed to care about is that the baby is healthy. Nope, not me. Because apparently I'm a jackass. So here's the part where you do NOT stop reading, so I can explain myself. Like if it's after midnight and your eyes are closing, hold them open with toothpicks or go lick the coffee filter from this morning or do something to keep yourself awake because I don't want you to go to sleep thinking about what a dickwad I am.

Okay, so flashback to 2011. We already have our cutie pie little girl and we are finally preggers with our second. Yippeeeee, a sibling is totally gonna make this shit easier. (See? I was a total dumbshit back then.) And it's time to go in for the big ultrasound. You know, the one where you find out what you're having.

HUBBY: Are you sure you don't want it to be a surprise this time?

ME: I do want it to be a surprise. When we find out from the ultrasound tech what it is.

HUBBY: But we found out the *first* time.

ME: When you're the one carrying a bowling ball in your belly and another one in your ass [hemorrhoid], then you get to decide.

Well, that shut him up. Seriously, if I'm ever a lesbian and my partner wants to carry the baby, she can totally decide that we're not finding out what we're having. I feel very comfortable making that promise. But I digress.

Anyways, the big ultrasound day comes and you can totally make fun of me for being all Pinterest-y and shit, but I bring two stuffed animals with me to the appointment (no, not to hug, I'm not a total loser). One is blue and the other is pink, and we have the tech secretly put the correct one in a box for us to take home so Zoey can open it tonight after dinner and we can have the silly surprise my hubby always wanted.

Okay, so if you haven't figured it out by now, I'm the kinda person who has ZERO willpower, which is why I drink a bottle of Hershey's syrup every night and chase it with giant fistfuls of Goldfish. So the second we get home, I put the box high up on a shelf where I can't reach it. But I keep seeing it out of the corner of my eye. Urrggghhh, I am sooooo tempted, I cannot begin to explain how much I want to pop open the flap of the box and take a quick peek. Pink or blue, pink or blue, pink or blue? I'm dying to know. Nooooo, don't do it, don't do it, don't do it.

Okay, this is not working, so I take out a roll of wrapping paper (black because that's all we have and I have no F'ing idea why we even have black wrapping paper because that's so weird) and I wrap it up. Yes, this is a great idea! Not only will it stop me from peeking all day, but it'll be even more fun for Zoey to open later. Much laaaater. This is ridiculous. I have a shitload of things to do today and there is no way I can get them done with this damn box staring at me.

ME: Honey!!! Zoey!! Come to the kitchen to open the surprise!!!

HUBBY: I thought we were going to do it after dinner.

ME: Then clearly you don't know me very well. Okay, Zoey, let's see if you're going to have a baby sister or a baby brother!!

FYI, she's not even two at the time and has no F'ing idea what I'm talking about, but we push record on the video camera and we let her unwrap the box. Eeeeeks, this is so exciting!!! I can't wait to see what we're having!!

I'd totally show you the video here, but (a) this is a book so I can't, and (b) you would probably die before it's over because that's how long it takes for her to unwrap it. I shit you not. Watching her open this thing is like watching paint dry after watching someone invent paint and then watching them build the entire paint factory and then watching them physically make the bucket of paint. Seriously, it could not take any longer for her to open it while my hubby and I sit there dyyying with anticipation.

IN UNISON: Come on, sweetie, you can do it.

IN OUR HEADS: RAWRRRRRR, just rip OFF the F'ING wrapping paper already!!!!!!

And after she manages to take all the wrapping paper off the box without tearing it at all, she takes about ten more minutes to get the flap open. I shit you not. I am seriously going to lose my mind.

ME: ARRGGHHH, JUST YANK THAT SHIT OPEN ALREADY!!!

And then I see it. The tip of a tiny little blue ear pops out of the box. You know that tightening feeling you get in your chest when something big happens? I get THAT feeling. Yup, I actually feel bad for a moment. Not terrible, but a little bummed. Which is so weird because I've always been the kind of person who says I don't care if it's a boy or a girl. But apparently I'm not the nice person I always thought I was. I'm an a-hole.

I mean boys scare the shit out of me. I don't know jack shit about boys. They're into trucks and ninja turtles and superheroes. Things I don't know about. And they have penises. I don't know what to do with that thing. Well, I know what to do with it if it's on a man, but not on a little boy. And people are always saying how wild boys are and how loud they are and I always see brothers wrestling and almost killing each other, and guess who become serial killers? Boys. You never hear about girl serial killers. Shit, I am totally going to raise a boy serial killer. This is not good. Not good at all.

Plus, all I can think about are those HUGE bins of adorable itty-bitty pink-and-white sundresses I had so carefully packed away in the basement. And the supercute pink polka-dot bedding set that I spent $300 on and loved so much, even though I could only use the fitted sheet because bumpers and comforters are basically baby murderers. And yes, I know I was an idiot for spending $300 on a bedding set, but I was preggers and certifiably crazy. And besides, if I use it again then I can basically divide that price in two and $150 for one fitted sheet doesn't sound nearly as bad. Kinda sorta.

But there it is. A little blue stuffed animal sitting there in the middle of the kitchen table and there's no changing it. And sure, I guess I can still use that hot pink bedding set because I don't want to condition him to like only "boy" colors, the same way I painted Zoey's room orange instead of pink or purple when she was a baby, but I'm pretty sure the hubby's not gonna go for that.

Anyways, my hubby is practically jizzing himself he's soooooo excited to have a boy, so I fake a big smile and pretend to be excited too. I mean wait, I am excited. It's not like I'm totally bumming inside. After all, *boy* was my second choice. But like I said, I'm also scared shitless.

Until the day I had him.

Cut to six months later in the hospital when I'm holding my new little tyke in my arms and I suddenly realize that everything the other mothers said is true. (a) You really *do* love your second baby as much as the first, and (b) holy crap are boys AWESOME. This baby is soooooo stinkin' cute I can barely handle it. Who cares if I screw up and raise him to be a serial killer?! He's cute enough to get away with it!

The second they put him in my arms, he's immediately my little buddy for life. And I can't stop kissing his sweet face. And OMG, look at his cute little package!! FYI, it's little because he's a baby, not because he isn't well-hung (I have no idea how hung he is because whenever one of my friends changes her son's diaper I do an extra good job at averting my eyes because I don't want anyone to think I'm a perv). And we put him in this adorable Superman shirt and it even has an itty-bitty cape on it. And later I put him in this sweet camouflage onesie. And ooooh, I can't believe they make teeny-tiny Vans that are like three inches long. Not that babies need shoes, but yes, he kinda needs Vans because they're too cute for words. Like him.

Why was I ever scared about having a boy?!! Boys rock!

DADDY: *Zoey, stop leaving the door open. The cat's gonna get out.*

ZOEY: *Yeah, I know. And then we can get a dog.*

ME: *Zoey, it's chilly. You have to wear pants.*

ZOEY: *No.*

ME: *Yes.*

ZOEY: *No.*

ME: *Yes. And don't say no to me.*

ZOEY: *Fine, then I'm wearing them like this.*

*And she did, all morning long. She showed me.
Annnnd everyone else. Awesome.*

Thinking outside
the penalty box

RIDDLE ME THIS, BATMAN. WTF do you do when you've given so many timeouts that your kid's butt has made a permanent impression in the carpet and he couldn't give a rat's ass if you put him in a penalty box again? I'll tell you what you do. You come up with some more creative ways to make him behave. Here's a little multiple choice quiz to see if you're thinking outside the box when it comes to punishing your turdmonsters.

If your kid is throwing a tantrum because apparently you weren't supposed to unwrap his granola bar for him, you:

A. Ignore it

B. Get him a new granola bar that he can unwrap himself

C. Shove the entire granola bar into your mouth right in front of him and chow down

THE CORRECT ANSWER IS C.

If you've told your daughter to put her shoes on 9,000 times and she still doesn't listen, you:

A. Ask her politely to use her ears

B. Use a Q-tip to make sure she doesn't have major wax buildup

C. Make her a hat she has to wear the rest of the day

THE CORRECT ANSWER IS C.

If your kids refuse to set the table, you:

A. Roll your eyes and set it yourself

B. Refuse to serve dinner until they set it and let the dinner get cold

C. Bring the entire pot of spaghetti and meatballs over to the table and scoop it out straight onto the table in front of each of them and tell them to eat that shit with their hands since they don't have silverware and that they're not getting up until they eat every last drop and clean up the mess

THE CORRECT ANSWER IS C.

If your kids keep fighting over a toy, you:

A. Try to teach them to take turns

B. Take the toy away and say no one gets it

c. Do this:

"I told you guys it would break if you didn't stop fighting over it."

THE CORRECT ANSWER IS C.

If your kid keeps asking for a toy over and over again at the store even though you've told her no a thousand times, you:

A. Explain to her that lots of girls and boys don't have any toys

B. Let her buy it with her piggy bank money

c. Put the toy in your cart and then pick up your phone and

call Santa right in front of her and inform him that she's hit
her toy quota and won't need a delivery this year

THE CORRECT ANSWER IS C.

If your kid keeps getting up from the dinner table, you:

A. Keep yelling at him to sit down

B. Take his food away even if he's not done

C. MAKE him stay seated

Heyyyy, look at that. Duct tape really does fix anything!

THE CORRECT ANSWER IS C.

If your ungrateful family keeps being jerkwads and forgetting to say thank you and basically treats you like a housekeeper, you:

A. Pour yourself a bottle of vino

B. Down it

C. Book a one-way ticket to the Caribbean and say you're not coming home until they start acting appreciative and the house better be clean when you get back

THE CORRECT ANSWER IS ALL OF THE ABOVE.

HOLDEN: *But I didn't want a pink balloon!*

(Pop!)

ME: *There you go. Now you don't have one.*

One of the worst
feelings in the world

THIS IS THE DAY EVERYTHING CHANGED. The day I lost Zoey.

The day started out like any other. It was drizzly so we took our kids to this indoor play place where they could climb in this cool tree house thingie while all the parents stood around and watched. Or if your kids are on the older side like ours and you don't have to worry about them being mowed down by big kids anymore, you stand there and stare at your cell phone and look up when they say, "Mom, look at me!" which only happens about once every .3 seconds.

Anyways, after an hour or so of looking up every .3 seconds to watch my daughter slide down a slide headfirst or my son stand on one foot (future Olympians in the making), it was time to go. I mean sure, we could have stayed there all day and they'd have been happy, but my stomach was literally about to eat itself because I stupidly thought it would be a good idea to have a healthy smoothie for breakfast instead of my usual four bowls of cereal.

ME: Can you give the kids a five-minute warning?

HUBBY: Sure.

(A few minutes later he came back.)

HUBBY: Have you seen Zoey?

ME: No. Did you tell her it's time to leave?

HUBBY: I tried to. I can't find her.

Now I don't know about your husband, but if I told my husband to go get some milk and he was literally standing on a dairy farm in front of a big jug of milk with the word *MILK* written in giant letters on the bottle and the milk could talk and it was saying, "I am the milk your wife wants you to get," my husband would still come back to me and say, "I can't find any milk." So let's just say I wasn't really alarmed.

ME: Did you look for her?

HUBBY: Yes.

ME: Like you *really* looked for her?

HUBBY: Yes.

ME: Maybe she's up there in that tree house section.

HUBBY: I looked.

ME: Did you try the ball section?

HUBBY: She's not there.

I mean seriously? Do I have to do *everything*?

I started scanning the play area for her purple dress. It's pretty easy to find because it's bright magenta and she's one of the older kids so she's a bigger surface area now. I walked closer to look in the punching bag area. Not there. I walked down to where the babies play. Zoey lovvvvvves babies. Not there either. I looked in the ball area. Nope. The more places I looked, the more I started to get a pit in my stomach. I started to look in less obvious places. Behind the couches? No. Hiding between the punching bags? Not there.

Oh my God. What if? No, she has to be somewhere. You just haven't found her yet. Try not to panic. But I was starting to panic. My hubby was looking for her too and he also looked worried. There was panic in his voice.

HUBBY: Zoey! Zoey!! ZOEY!!!

He's not the one who usually panics. That's my role. But he was panicking and that made me even more afraid. It's like when I fly on an airplane and if there's turbulence and I see a flight attendant looking freaked out, I'm like, oh shit, we're totally going down. Shit. Shit. Shit. Oh my God, we've lost her. I couldn't believe this was happening. This was that moment in your life that you can look back on and say, that was the moment everything changed.

I saw a reading area and thought, of course, she loves books, but when I got closer, all I saw was one little blonde girl reading by herself.

GIRL: She's not heeeere.

Like she was straight out of a horror movie. Oh wait, the bathroom! Yes, I'll bet she really had to go and went in quickly without telling us so I barged inside and saw another mom in there.

ME: Have you seen a little girl with a purple dress?

RANDOM MOM: Nope. *(to her kid)* How did you get this applesauce all over you?

KID: I don't know.

Agghhhhh, who cares about your stupid applesauce?!! My kid is missing!!!!

HUBBY: Not in the bathroom?

ME: Go tell them at the front desk.

He hesitated.

ME: NOW!

It's time to full-on panic.

HOLDEN: Mommy?

I looked down and saw Holden standing there and I suddenly felt terrible for him. What if this is it? What if he's an only child now? Don't think that way, don't think that way, don't think that way. But I couldn't help it. I scooped him up and started looking for Zoey again.

My heart was in my throat and I felt like I should be crying but my eyes were totally dry. It was like I was too scared to cry. I scanned the room again. It had been at least ten minutes now, a long F'ing time when you are looking for a responsible girl in a single room that has no walls where it shouldn't be hard to find someone. Like there was enough time to think about all sorts of scary shit I've seen on *Criminal Minds* and *Law & Order* and *America's Most Wanted* and James Patterson novels and pretty much any abduction story I'd ever seen before. It was horrifying. One of the people who worked there came up to me looking way too relaxed.

WORKER: What is your daughter wearing?

ME: A purple dress. Magenta.

WORKER: Don't worry, she didn't leave here. We watch the door carefully.

Really? Because you're standing here with me right now and I can see that no one is at the door.

ME: Do something!

WORKER: She's gotta be somewhere.

Yeah, in the men's restroom with a pedophile. Or in a stranger's car. Or chloroformed and in their trunk. DO SOMETHING NOW!!!!

I turned away from Miss Nonchalancy and started looking for the two kids Zoey was playing with earlier. The girl in the rainbow shirt and the boy with the iPad. Maybe they would know where she is. I didn't see them anywhere. I didn't see their mom either. Oh my God, what if they took her? She wouldn't go with a stranger but she's been playing with them the whole time. Maybe she thinks they're not strangers. Plus, they had an iPad. She would follow anyone with an iPad. And the mother did look a little odd.

I couldn't believe this was happening. This couldn't be happening. What if she's gone? I can't even—

And then suddenly I saw something out of the corner of my eye. I saw something magenta pop out of the bottom of the twisty tube slide. Oh my God, it's her. Thank you. Thank you. Thank you. I felt silly for panicking. I felt embarrassed for getting upset with the worker. But can you blame me? Isn't this how it happens when a child gets kidnapped? The panic is slow. People assume the kid is just hiding, that the parents are panicking for no reason. People don't take it seriously at first, and then eventually after looking in every nook and cranny, they start to realize that this is real. That a child is missing. Like really missing.

My hubby got to Zoey first. He wrapped his arms around her and then I saw him talking to her seriously. Turns out she had been sitting inside the middle of the twisty tube slide the whole time. Like smack in the middle of it. Just sitting there. Letting other kids go over her. For like ten minutes. I wanted to kiss her. I wanted to hug her. I wanted to beat the crap out of her. I leaned over and kissed her awkwardly because my hubby was still holding her. And then I told her to never do that again. NEVER. EVER.

She could see the look in our eyes. How serious we were. How scared we were.

ZOEY: I'm sorry.

ME: It's okay. *(deep breath out)*

ZOEY: Phew, Mom. That was a close one.

Holy crap, kiddo. You have no idea.

MOM'S swear jar

damn- 5¢
Shit - 10¢
fuck - 25¢

Kids' swear jar

MOMMMYY - 5¢
MOMMMMYYY - 10¢
MOMMY, MOMMY,
MOMMY, MOMMY- 25¢

One fish, two fish, red fish, gross fish

OKAY, SO I FEEL LIKE WHENEVER WE GO ON VACATION, there's always that one magical moment (of course, once you have kids, it's sandwiched between 10,000 shitty moments). Like when my hubby and I went on our honeymoon, there was this time our sailboat was surrounded by hundreds of spinner dolphins leaping out of the water all around us. Or the time we went to the Dominican Republic and my masseuse full-on massaged my boobs. It was a couple's massage and I was dying to yell to my hubby who was lying next to me with his eyes closed, "Look, she's rubbing my nipples!!!" Or the time we went to Florida and this happened.

We were walking down the beach with the kiddos when suddenly there was all this bright silver flashing all over the surface of the water. Everyone on the beach literally stopped what they were doing and watched together. "Look, there it is!" And then it stopped, and then it was there again, and then it stopped, and then it was there again, and so on and so on. It took us all about thirty seconds to figure out what we were seeing.

It was thousands of flying fish (I have no idea what kind of fish they really were, but they looked like they were flying). Over and over again they'd leap out of the water in big groups moving down the shoreline for like 10 minutes straight as everyone stood there mesmerized.

And then when it was done we all looked down at our feet and realized that something sucky had also happened. A bunch of those fish had jumped wayyyy too close to the shore and when the waves went out, they were left stranded on the beach, dying.

Wahhh, poor little fishy.

But hey, I'm a big believer in letting nature take its course and survival of the fittest and all that other Darwin crap, so I'm like, sucks to be you. See ya. And I started to walk away.

And that's when I looked up and saw Zoey's face. She was devastated.

ZOEY: Mommm, they're dying.

ME: I know, honey. It's sad.

ZOEY: We have to save them.

Uhhh, yeahhh, you do that. 'Cause my fingers don't touch slimy shit from the ocean. Especially when it's still alive and staring up at me with its little beady eye.

ME: Go ahead. Toss them back in.

And that's when she looked up at me with tears in her eyes and I don't think in her entire life have I ever seen her look sooooo sad. She couldn't bring herself to pick it up.

ZOEY: I can't do it.

ME: Yes, you can.

ZOEY: *(sobbing)* No, I can't.

Well, why *would* she be able to do it? Here she is watching her mom be a lame-ass chicken shit, so where would she get the courage to do it? If I didn't touch the fish, I wasn't just failing as an AROS (Animal Rescue Operation Specialist) (yes, I made that shit up). I was failing as Zoey's role model. Uggggh.

Deep breath in. Okay, here goes. Ewwwwwww. As I picked up the slimy fish between my two fingers, I prayed it wouldn't start flopping around in my hand. And then I ran with it as fast as humanly possible and tossed it back into the ocean.

ME: Swim, little guy, SWIM!!!!!

FYI, I didn't actually say that last part out loud, but if they make this into a Lifetime movie, the actress playing me (Eva Longoria/Kerry Washington/Megan Fox) totally would. But I digress.

You should have seen Zoey's face. There really is no word that captures the elation she felt at that moment. But there were still tons of fish all stranded along the beach. And she still hadn't done anything besides watch me.

ME: Come on, Zoey. Help me.

ZOEY: I can't.

ME: *(I stare straight into her eyes and use my deep James Earl Jones voice.)* Yes. You. Can.

And at that moment, she pulled together as much courage as she could and she slowly leaned down and her fingers touched the fish at her feet. It was fast and there's no way in hell she would actually pick it up by herself, but she did it. She touched it!!!

ZOEY: I did it!!!

ME: You did it! Come on, help me! Hold on to my wrist and you're saving it too!!

Kinda sorta.

And together we tossed like ten more fish back into the ocean. And after it was all over, Zoey celebrated touching a fish.

Before I became a mom, I knew I'd have to make all sorts of sacrifices. I'd have to stop going out as much at night. I'd have to stop listening to rap music in the car. I'd have to watch crappy TV shows (of course, I had no idea HOW bad, cough cough, *Caillou*). I even knew I'd have to touch totally gross things like poop and blood and vomit. But

never did I think that being a good mom would require me to pick up a live fish.

I guess that's what being a parent is about. Doing a lot of shit you never knew you'd have to do. And sometimes being a kickass parent isn't about being proud of your kiddo. Sometimes it's about being proud of yourself.

Okay, don't worry. I'm turning back into my normal cynical self now.

AWWW SHIT,
Whatta You Mean They Grow Up??

WHOA WHOA WHOA, WTF JUST HAPPENED?
Yesterday the nurses were wiping that gross cottage cheese stuff off my newborn and today she's graduating from kindergarten. Like remember in *Star Wars* how Han Solo could press that crazy little button on his dashboard and his rocket ship would suddenly launch into warp speed and shoot through space narrowly missing asteroids and shit? That's my life now. Constantly. One day I'm popping out babies and the next day my eggs are so rotten they smell like a sulfuric science experiment. Can someone pleeeease slow this ride down?!! And what really sucks is that there are people all over the world rubbing it in. Like whenever I walk down the street with my family, some random schmuckwad feels the need to tell me to appreciate my kids now because it goes by so quickly. I'm like, no shit, Sherlock. I feel how fast it's going. Yesterday she was in diapers and today she's wearing a thong. Not really, but she's wearing her underwear backward on purpose and that's very thong-like. Anyways, I'm stocking up on shitloads of alcohol for the day they leave me, which at this rate is going to be tomorrow.

If you have a vajayjay and she has a vajayjay, you're on the same team

Dear Zoey,

Here's the thing. I don't really give a shit what you are in life. You wanna be a prison guard? Awesome. You wanna be a drug dealer? As long as cannabis is legal in your state, deal away. You wanna be a proctologist? Gross, but whatever floats your boat.

I don't care WHAT you are, but I do care WHO you are. Especially when it comes to the way you treat other girls.

Look in your pants. See that thing in there. That is your vajay-jay. And anyone else that has one of those is on the same team. Capeesh? I know that life is hard right now, trying to decide important shit like should you watch PAW Patrol or Scooby-Doo, but believe it or not, life's gonna get even more complicated as you get older. And here are a few guidelines to remember when you're figuring out how to treat other girls:

1. *Never ever* EVER *step on another girl to climb higher socially. Girls are not rungs on a ladder. They are pillars. Pillars who will stand next to you and hopefully lend support when you desperately need it. And you* will *need it.*

2. *Do* NOT *make fun of other girls for their body parts. If they're too fat, if they're too skinny, if they have a mustache, if they have Fred Flintstone toes, if they get boobs before anyone else in your class, etc., etc., etc. Because remember, if she's the first girl to get boobs, that means you don't have them yet. And you could be the last girl to get boobs, and that's gonna suck even worse.*

3. *Here are four words I* NEVER *want you to say in the school cafeteria:* This seat is saved. *Oh, and here are six MORE words I never want you to say:* I'm sorry, this seat is saved. *Because only a-holes save seats. And even if you say it nicely, you're still just an a-hole saying it nicely.*

4. *If you are in the bathroom and another girl needs a tampon, give it to her. That's girl code. I don't care if she's your worst enemy and has a voodoo doll of you that she stabs every night. (a) Maybe she'll stop stabbing the voodoo doll, and (b) if you mess with girl code, karma comes back to bite you in the ass with a vengeance.*

5. *Girls are like totally good at saying bad shit behind each other's backs. But friends are like totally good at ignoring that shit and staying out of those conversations. There is only one time it's okay to talk behind a friend's back: if you are planning a surprise party for her.*

6. *Remember, the group of girls you go to prom with is just as important as the boy you go to prom with. Maybe even more so. Because there's a good chance you aren't gonna marry your date, but it's quite possible you'll keep those girl friends for the rest of your life.*

7. *Speaking of boys, it's not a competition to see which girl can win the boy. It's a competition to see which girl can be the most kickass, awesome, self-confident girl, and then the right boy will come.*

8. *If one of your girl friends gets super drunk and does lots of stupid stuff, don't make fun of her. Be there for her. To hold back her hair, to get her home safely, to keep watch while she pees in an alley, to give her a glass of water, to stop her from giving BJs to the whole football team, to talk to her about it the next day, to never mention it again. She made a mistake. Your job as a friend is to keep her from making more mistakes.*

9. *Don't change to be like the other girls. Unless you're being a douchebag and they're being nice, in which case change to be like them.*

10. *Usually I tell you that school is the most important thing, but this time I won't. Girl friends are. You are more likely to retain your girl friends twenty years from now than any lesson you learned in history class, so treat them like gold.*

Damn straight. Anyone kums in my daughter's room and we're gonna have a serious problem.

Dear lady I just saw breastfeeding at a restaurant

Really? Do you seriously have to pick the table right in front of me so I have to stare at you the whole time you do THAT? I mean yeah, I guess I could pick up and move to a different table, but F that, I was here first.

And now I have to sit here staring at you breastfeeding for God knows how long because you insist on doing it in public. And here's why I think that is so wrong.

Because now I have to listen to that cute little baby suckle away at you like you're the best thing on earth. Now I have to stare at those adorable little hands reaching out from under your Hooter Hider or Boobie Blanket or Coconut Concealer or whatever all the new moms are wearing these days. And now I have to watch you kiss those itty-bitty toes that are like the size of Tic Tacs, and wahhh, I'll never have toes like that to kiss again. You're totally rubbing it in.

I mean these days if I try to kiss my kiddos' toes, I either get a giant whiff of nasty foot odor or they're like, WTF, Mom, and kick me in the face. And besides, have you seen my kids' feet? Hellll-looo, toe cheese and sock lint and black dirt in every crevice. No, thank you.

I know you have no idea I'm even watching you because you're lost in your own little world with your brand-new perfect new-born, but quit being so selfish and think about other people for once. People like me who are positive we don't want to have any more rugrats, until someone like you parks yourself and your porn-star tatas right in front of us. I mean I know we're sup-posed to avert our eyes, but it's hard not to sneak a peek when your little love muffin keeps making all those adorable cooing noises.

To think there was a time in my life that I thought breast-feeding was a pain and wanted to be done with it. What was I thinking? Because you know what's harder than breastfeeding? When your daughter doesn't want to kiss you good-bye because her friends are watching. Or when your son won't let you carry him anymore and insists on doing everything by himself. Or when both of your kids go to camp for the first time and suddenly you're sitting there in the kitchen all alone and you're like now what?

Anyways, how dare you breastfeed in front of me and rub it in my face and make me wish my kiddos were babies again and make my uterus do the come-on-let's-have-another-baby *dance. Before you sat down, I was 100% sure I was done. And now I'm only 99% sure. And I know that doesn't seem like a big amount, but that 1% makes all the difference.*

So yeah, I know there are all these crazy people out there who say breastfeeding in public should be outlawed because it's ugly, but I think it should be outlawed because it's beautiful.

Next time, please be a little more considerate and take your breastfeeding somewhere else.

> *Sincerely,*
> *A mom who didn't want more kids . . .*
> *until you sat down*

HOLDEN: *Look how big my belly is!!*

ME: *Wow! Do you have a baby in your belly?*

(Oh shit, I shouldn't have said that. Now he's totally gonna think boys can get pregnant.)

HOLDEN: *Yeah, it's a girl baby!!*

ME: *That's funny, buddy, but you know only women can get pregnant, right?*

HOLDEN: *No, boys can too.*

ME: *Nope, buddy, only a woman can have a baby in her belly.*

HOLDEN: *No.*

ME: *Yes.*

HOLDEN: *No.*

ME: *Yes.*

HOLDEN: *No. What if a boy EATS a baby? Then he can have a baby in his belly.*

Touché, Holden. Of course, he'd also go to prison for cannibalism, but yes, he would have a baby in his belly.

I couldn't make this shit up if I tried.

ZOEY: *Mama, am I getting boobs?*

Well, this is just awesome. It's only day three of the first grade and Zoey has learned soooo much already. At this rate I'll be explaining doggy style to her before the holiday break.

Twelve things I will always miss about being preggers

YEAH, I KNOW WHAT YOU'RE THINKING. WHAT?!! Who the hell misses being pregnant? Well, I do. I mean no, I don't miss the hemorrhoids and the sciatica and the constipation and the lack of sleep and the back pain and the night sweats and the inability to tie my shoelaces, etc., etc., etc., but other than a few thousand bad symptoms, I LOVED being pregnant. I mean, how cool is that? You're growing a real live human being in your belly. It's like science fiction! But alas, I'm forty-two, I have all the kiddos I want, and I'll never do it again. So here goes. Twelve things I will always miss about being preggers:

1. Feeling a tiny little baby moving around inside me. Wahhh, I'll never feel that again. And then one day I get a little gas bubble and it feels just like I have a baby in there and for a moment I'm like, "Eeeeks, I just felt him kick!" and then I remember nope, I just had Chipotle for lunch.

2. Having a ridiculously full head of awesome hair. Sure, it sucks balls when it all falls out after and my bathroom looks like I live with a long-haired orangutan, but for nine short months

I walked around flipping my hair like I was in a Pantene commercial.

3. My hubby doting on me. Because unless you're Britney Spears, there is only one time in your life when you can tell someone to hurry up and pinch the loaf on the toilet because you need Cherry Garcia and you need it NOWWWW.

4. Saying I'm eating for two. When I was preggers, I could literally wear a bag of Doritos like a feedbag around my neck and no one could judge me. Well, maybe they judged me but I didn't give a rat's ass because "the baby wanted it."

5. Seeing cool shit like a foot or an elbow moving around under my skin. I'm like, "Holy crap, honey, did you see that?!! Go grab the mini Vans so I can see if they're gonna fit!"

6. *Ding! You've got mail. Your baby is now the size of a plumcot!* And yeah, I have to google "plumcot" because I have no idea WTF that is, but I don't care because I lovvvve getting that email from BabyCenter every week.

7. Having a big awesome belly to rest shit on. My hands, my nachos, my can of soda that I shouldn't be drinking, my iPad, the remote, etc., etc., etc. And then after I have my baby, I'm standing at a party going, "Where the hell do I put my hands now?" So I cross my arms but then I just look all closed off and bitchy. In my pockets? No, that's weird. Fine, I'll just let my arms dangle by my sides like two fat salamis hanging at the deli. Perfect.

8. Having totally big awesome amazing porno boobs. Oh how I miss standing in front of the mirror topless and drooling and wondering whether I might be a narcissistic lesbian.

9. Never feeling cold. Like seriously, the only time in my life that I didn't have to carry a cardigan around with me wherever I go was when I was pregnant.

10. Maternity pants!!!! Maternity pants F'ing rock because they are soooo comfy and now the only day that it's acceptable for me to wear them is Thanksgiving. Grrrrr.

11. Having the perfect excuse not to have sex. "But honey, if we have sex your penis is going to be poking the baby in the head over and over again. And you don't want to have twins, do you?"

12. The excitement of knowing that I am *this close* to meeting the tiny, adorable, wonderful, amazing human being that we just created. Seriously, you could tell me I'm going to meet the president of the United States, the Queen of England, God himself, John Lennon, and J. K. Rowling all in one day, and it still wouldn't be as exciting as knowing I'm about to meet my new little baby.

HOLDEN: *Mom, maybe I can be a fairy when I grow up.*

WHAT I THINK: *Oh noooo, you're totally going to get picked on. Isn't life hard enough already? Wouldn't you rather play football? No wait, not football. Pick a less contact-y sport, like swimming or waterskiing. On second thought, nothing where you might drown or get eaten by a shark. What about the marching band? But not drums. I don't want to listen to drums. And not the trombone. Or the flute. Shit, forget instruments. Wrestling? Cauliflower ear. Chess? Too nerdy. Golf? BO-ring. Oh I know, tennis! Tennis is awesome! Yes, you'll be a great tennis player.*

WHAT I SAY: *Kiddo, you can be whatever you want to be. And if that's a fairy, you're gonna be the best damn Tinker Bell there ever was.*

Just a little sumpin' sumpin'
I had Zoey sign
before she could read

It is hereby agreed that this contract shall be entered into be-tween the parents, <u>Karen and Greg Alpert</u>, and the child, <u>Zoey Alpert</u>, on the 24th day of February, 2015, and that this contract will bind the parties by law and may not be broken for the rest of eternity under penalty of death. I, <u>Zoey Alpert</u>, agree to the following:

I agree to always let my parents hug and kiss me as much as they want and I will never wipe off their kisses no matter how wet they are.

I agree to always spend my birthday with my mother because really it should be her who is celebrated on that day.

I agree to never ever get a tattoo, unless of course it's the words "I love Mom" in a location that only my mother will see.

I agree to work ridiculously hard in high school so I can brag that I got into Harvard and Princeton but go to the amazing college down the street from my family.

I agree to let my parents interview not just the person I want to marry but their whole entire family as well so they can decide whether they are acceptable in-laws and they will have full veto power. If they veto said marriage, I agree to not throw a shit fit and I will thank them profusely for saving me from total self-destruction.

I agree never to look at the caller ID on my phone or wristwatch or ear microchip or whatever communication device people are using in that decade and let it go to voicemail if my parents are calling.

I agree never to expose my chest to get cheap plastic beads. If I really want some cheap plastic beads, I will call my mom and ask her to buy me some at Michaels.

I agree to always talk to my mom about boys or girls or whomever I'm into over a pint of ice cream with two spoons just like they do on TV.

I agree to let my father walk me down the aisle with the understanding that he is not "giving" me away, but rather loaning me out and can easily take me back if he deems it necessary.

I agree to grow up and have lots of adorable little squishy babies who I will gladly let my mom squish anytime she wants.

I agree to do my best to purchase a house that comes up for sale one day on my parents' street. It doesn't have to be visible from where they live, but walking distance would be ideal.

If I ever win an Oscar or an Olympic medal or the Super Bowl or something else amazing, I agree to thank my parents before I thank anyone else. Yes, even God.

I agree that the only naked pictures that will ever be taken of my bum are the ones my mom took when I was a baby.

I agree to always come to my parents if I'm in trouble, even if it means I will be in more trouble.

I agree to call my parents if I ever need to be bailed out of jail.

I agree to never need to be bailed out of jail.

I agree to love and cherish my mom and dad no matter what, even once I can read and understand this contract and realize what they had me sign.

I agree to never sign another contract without reading it first.

X _____ZOEY_____ date _2|24/17_

The last chapter

Dear Friend,

Yup, as far as I'm concerned anyone who reads my whole book is officially one of my friends. Like if you came up to me right now, I would put on a shirt that says "my friend" with an arrow pointing at you. And if two people came up to me and said they read my book, I would keep spinning around so the arrow would always be pointing at one of them. And if a whole crowd of people came up to me and said they read my book, I would probably jizz in my pants. But I digress.

Anyways, thank you. Thanks for reading this. Thanks for telling other people to read it and not just loaning them your copy because you know you read some of it in the bathroom and then you would just be handing your friend a book that's covered in poo particles. And most of all, thanks for being another kickass mediocre parent. I mean sometimes with all the Pinterest-y posts and Facebook brags I see out there, I feel like I must be the worst parent on earth. But then I look around and I see all of you guys hanging out in your elastic waistband pants and dirty minivans and greasy ponytails and I'm like, ohhhh, there are so many of us mediocre parents!! Which makes US the normal ones. Yayyyy!! Power in numbers!

So the next time Judy Judgypoo looks down her nose at you because your Tasmanian devil is throwing a tantrum in the middle of the shopping mall and hers looks like an angel without a hair out of place, try to remember, you're the normal one. And her kid will probably rebel one day and do a lot of drugs and become a hooker. I mean I don't really know that for sure, but I'm optimistic.

Or the next time Muffy McPerfectpants judges you for feeding your kids Happy Meals or soda pop or both at the same time (GASP!!), here's what I want you to do. I want you to grab a fist-ful of those French fries and shove them into your pie-hole right in front of her face and say, "Nom nom nom, man does that di-methylpolysiloxane tastes deeeelish." And then deal with the repercussions of your rugrat, who's probably FREAKING out be-cause you stole some of his stupid French fries that YOU paid for that he's not gonna finish anyways.

And last but not least, walk away holding your head up high. Higher than hers. Even if she's wearing four-inch Louboutins and you're wearing slippers. Because you, my friend, rock the Casbah.

Now please excuse me while I go check on my rugrats. Leaving them unattended while I sat in the shitter and wrote this book may not have been the best idea. It's a little disconcerting that I haven't heard from them for a few days. Ruh-roh.

Signing off with a big ole crotch-to-crotch hug and not one of those wussy hugs where people stand a foot away from each other and barely touch.

xoxoxoxoxoxoxoxo,
The crazy lady who wrote this book

Acknowledgments

FIRST AND FOREMOST, I'd like to thank my family for being ridiculously awesome. Life would be so boring without you. Thank you for giving me the material to write about and thanks for putting up with me while I wrote this book and was stressed out beyond belief and turned into a mega bitch. And speaking of people who put up with my shit, thanks to my illustrator, Lyssa Bowen, who didn't laugh in my face or push back at all when I asked her to do all sorts of annoying things like redraw all of the characters with different eyebrows and then after she did it changed my mind and asked her to do it again but to go back to the original eyebrows but this time to try adding mustaches to all of them so we can see what that looks like. I'd also like to thank my agent, Rachel Sussman, who totally kicks ass and answers all of my stupid questions and I'm sure she's reading this right now saying, "Your questions aren't stupid, Karen," even though they totally are. I'd like to profusely thank my editors at HarperCollins, Amy Bendell and Lisa Sharkey, and my editorial assistant, Alieza Schvimer, who all gave me the most awesome feedback and helped me polish this turd into a lemon and then turn that lemon into lemonade. Plus, a huge-ass thank you to everyone else at HarperCollins who worked on this book. Without you, I would be nothing but a self-published author doing this all alone and I've done that before and holy crap was it hard, so thank you for everything you do. And, of course, thank you to anyone who's reading this book and actually reading the acknowledgments section. You F'ing rock. That or you're just bored out of your mind and don't have anything better to do. And last but not least, a big ole humungous thank you to my own parents, who I'm sure have wanted an epidural many, *MANY* times since they had me.